They look identical, but—

Theresa Joan is:

A flirt

A dynamo

The kind of woman every man wants

Theresa Jean is:

Hardworking

Loyal

The kind of woman every man wants...
as a friend

But now, Theresa Jean *is* Theresa Joan, and the fun is just beginning! Confused? So is Christopher MacAffee.

Valentine's Day is just around the corner and he's just fallen for the perfect woman...but he has no idea who she is!

Dear Reader,

Happy Valentine's Day! I hope you are enjoying a happy and romantic month.

Harlequin is romance, so February 14 is an extraspecial day for us. Some people say it with flowers, others with chocolates, others with expensive jewelry, but those three little words, *I love you,* are perhaps the best words in our vocabulary. And at Harlequin, we get to be part of this experience all year long!

As a treat for this special day, what better way to recall the joy of falling in love, than with our Love & Laughter selection this month. RITA Award-winning author Marie Ferrarella spins a delightfully comic tale of identical cousins (they walk alike, they talk alike...) and the man who doesn't know which woman he's in love with! Talented newcomer Stephanie Bond hits a hilarious note in *Irresistible?* Single and dateless Ellie Sutherland, who considers Valentine's Day *Black Friday* (I know those of you who are single on Valentine's Day can relate!), takes *scientific* action to land a man.

Wishing you much love—and laughter,

Malle Vallik

Malle Vallik
Associate Senior Editor

MY PHONY VALENTINE

Marie Ferrarella

Harlequin Books

TORONTO • NEW YORK • LONDON
AMSTERDAM • PARIS • SYDNEY • HAMBURG
STOCKHOLM • ATHENS • TOKYO • MILAN
MADRID • WARSAW • BUDAPEST • AUCKLAND

ISBN 0-373-44013-8

MY PHONY VALENTINE

This edition published by arrangement with Harlequin Books S.A.

Printed in U.S.A.

It's both touching and ironic that I should be tapped to write a book about Valentine's Day. Valentine's Day has always been a very special day to me, but in a Charlie Brown sort of way. A romantic from the moment I let out my first howl on Easter Sunday (no, I won't tell you what year—I mentally update it each year, anyway), I always dreamed of getting a card from that "special someone." Never mind that the other three hundred and sixty-four days of the year there *was* no "special someone"—I was convinced he was going to make his appearance on Valentine's Day. And of course, "he" never did. If it weren't for the fact that for the first six years of our school life, the teacher forcibly makes people drop valentines into your envelope (or box, or whatever), and the fact that I had a very understanding mother, I would have never even held a valentine in my hand.

My first voluntary valentine came from the man I wound up marrying (he had other attributes, too, besides card sending), so in essence, the card was worth waiting for. Just like T.J.'s wait for that "special someone" in *My Phony Valentine* was worth the effort.

I wish you all special valentines in your lives (just not mine, he's busy).

Love,

Marie Ferrarella

Marie Ferrarella has written more than seventy books for Harlequin and Silhouette. Don't miss these exciting, upcoming titles: *Traci on the Spot* from Silhouette Yours Truly in March 1997, *Your Baby or Mine?* from Silhouette Romance in April 1997 and *The Amnesiac Bride* from Silhouette Intimate Moments in June 1997.

To Helen Conrad,
for friendship, for listening, and for the title

1

"I WANT YOU to be me."

T.J. stared at the telephone receiver in her hand, stunned.

It wasn't until the telephone on her desk had rung three times that Theresa Jean Cochran had even become aware of it. With her mind on the statistics she'd pulled up on the screen, T.J. had groped for the receiver, managed to hit the speaker button instead and mumbled a preoccupied "hello."

"T.J."

Theresa *Joan* Cochran's voice had filled her cousin T.J.'s sun-bathed seventh-floor corner office. Uncertainty had nudged at T.J. as she'd glanced at the telephone. Why was Theresa calling her on the phone? Why hadn't she just swept in without knocking, the way she normally did? It never occurred to Theresa that she had to knock. As the president of C & C Advertising, she was accustomed to going anywhere she chose within the three floors that the agency occupied in the Endicott building—short of perhaps the men's room. And entrance into the latter might have been ventured on a dare. So far, no one had wanted to see just how far the flamboyant executive would go if challenged.

Even if Theresa hadn't been the head of the company her grandfather had founded and her father had so diligently developed into a top advertising firm, she would have felt absolutely no compunction about invading her cousin's space. It was something Theresa had been doing with fair regularity ever since they had been children. By now, it was as natural to her as breathing.

T.J., named after the same paternal grandmother Theresa had been, had reached for the receiver then. Light was flooding in through the two adjacent windows behind her, but the office had suddenly seemed chilly, as a feeling of déjà vu waltzed through her, doing double time.

She was more than familiar with the tone her cousin was using. Theresa was out for something. Like as not, it was a favor. A teeny-tiny little favor.

It was always some "teeny-tiny little favor" that would somehow snowball, embedding T.J. along with it as it built up momentum. When they were children, some of the favors had been pretty outrageous, but of late, they usually involved work, one account or another that had to be diplomatically rescued after being in the path of Hurricane Theresa. That was the name some of the older employees had pinned on her behind her back.

T.J. suspected that Theresa was aware of the nickname and took it to be a compliment.

They'd been born nine months apart, with T.J. the senior; it was Theresa who was the flashy, outgoing one. Theresa who was constantly being photographed as she was squired around by one after another of the country's most eligible bachelors. And it was T.J. who burned the midnight oil at the company. T.J. who was by far the creative force that propelled them into new contracts and new accounts and who helped cement the old ones by breathing new life into them.

Which was fine with T.J. She preferred remaining in the shadows and doing something she considered worthwhile and creative. T.J. had always enjoyed pulling her weight. Theresa enjoyed pulling off coups. They worked well together.

Because the computer was too slow for her taste, T.J. had pressed two buttons to automatically save her work. Bracing herself, she had taken a deep breath. She'd had a feeling this was going to take a while.

"To what do I owe this pleasure?" T.J. had looked at her watch. It was going on to nine o'clock. She wondered if Theresa was still home. It wouldn't be the first time Theresa was late.

She'd heard Theresa sigh dramatically. No one could sigh dramatically like Theresa. This had the makings of something big.

"T.J., I need help."

T.J. had leaned back in her chair. Yup, big. "Help as in help with a campaign, help with an ad idea or..." Her voice had trailed off, waiting for Theresa to fill in the proper ending.

Theresa had picked none of the above. And that was when she had laid the bomb at her feet and said, "I want you to be me."

T.J. now raised her brows. Bangs the color of milk chocolate threatened to mingle with dusky eyelashes. "That wasn't going to be my next guess." Not at this point in their lives, anyway.

Theresa didn't seem to hear her. It was a habit she had long honed to perfection, shutting out everything that didn't mesh with what she was thinking. "You're the perfect choice, T.J."

Not for nothing was she called Hurricane Theresa, T.J. thought. T.J., on the other hand, liked things spelled out and neatly organized.

"I think I missed a step here, Theresa. I'm a little slow before my fourth cup of coffee." Forsaking the computer entirely, she gave her undivided attention to the woman on the telephone. "Fill in the gaps for me, will you?"

There was a long pause, as if Theresa was searching for the right words. This probably had to do with conducting some meeting for her, T.J. mused. If she knew her cousin, there was a slope out there that needed skiing, or a man who needed her company at some secluded cabin hideaway. That left her to tie up ends for Theresa. Her cousin had a unique way of keeping a thriving business going while having a hell of a good time herself—elsewhere.

But Theresa was gorgeous and charming and rich, so everyone forgave her. In that respect, T.J. was no different from anyone else. And in T.J.'s case, there was also the matter of genuine affection and a sense of protectiveness that, if Theresa had thought about it, would have made her laugh in delighted amazement.

T.J. decided to prod Theresa along. "Why would I have to be you when you can be you so much better?" T.J. wanted to get to the end of the riddle before she grew too old to make sense of it.

"That's just the problem. I can't. I'm in the hospital."

T.J. bolted to attention. "In the hospital? Oh, God,

Theresa, are you all right?'' She began searching with her bare feet for her shoes under the desk. ''What hospital are you in? I'll be right there.'' She drove too fast. Theresa always drove too fast. Why didn't she ever listen to her and slow—

''No, don't. I'm okay, really. But the car isn't.'' Theresa's voice sobered. ''It's totaled. And it was such a beautiful shade of blue, too.''

T.J. ran her hand over her face. If Theresa could express sorrow over the loss of a car, then she was probably all right. T.J. took in a cleansing breath and let it out slowly, calming down. She needed facts. ''You were in a car accident?''

''It wasn't my fault.'' Theresa's voice was tinged with a note of defensiveness. ''The other car ran a light.''

Maybe, maybe not. What mattered now was Theresa. ''But you're sure you're all right?''

''Of course I'm sure. But the doctors are being difficult.'' T.J. could visualize the pout on Theresa's face as she said that. She wasn't accustomed to taking orders. ''They want to keep me here for observation. Of course,'' she continued, her voice becoming loftier, ''there's this one who I wouldn't mind having examine me by candlelight....''

Theresa was fine, T.J. thought with relief. ''You're digressing.''

''Right as always.'' Assured of her audience and the response, Theresa pushed forward. ''I need you to be me with Christopher MacAffee.''

''Christopher MacAffee, as in MacAffee Toys?''

''Yes.''

A copy of the presentation T.J. had labored over

for the man was housed on the blue disk on her desk. She'd scanned her hand-drawn sketches in just last night. Christopher MacAffee was the newly appointed president of MacAffee Toys, taking the position over from his ailing father. MacAffee Toys was a hundred-and-twenty-year-old toy manufacturing company that had managed to hang on to integrity as well as healthy profits through several generations.

But knowing all this still didn't answer any of the questions that were crowding T.J.'s brain. "You're losing me again."

"Christopher MacAffee is coming down this afternoon to meet with me about finalizing the account. He has some questions about the presentation. You worked on the campaign," Theresa reminded her needlessly.

Some of her best work had gone into that campaign. "Yes?"

"You know how stuffy that man is."

Actually, T.J. thought, she had no idea how stuffy the man was or wasn't. She had dealt only with his production assistant, and then only by telephone, but she said nothing as Theresa continued.

"He is completely inflexible about his policies and he insists on only dealing with the head man—or head *woman* in this case."

Despite Theresa's sometimes capricious nature, T.J. knew that her cousin took pride in the fact that she was the head of a large, respected advertising firm. An advertising firm with a quality reputation.

A sinking feeling was beginning to take hold. T.J. felt herself being drawn in. "And you want me to go in your place. Completely. Not just represent you but *be* you?''

''You have to.''

''Theresa, I don't have to do anything but raise Megan, pay taxes and die.'' Now there was a pretty thought, T.J. mused. But there were times when her cousin got her frustrated. And she really didn't like the idea of trying to fool the president of a large company whose account they were courting.

''T.J., I know what this is about. You don't have any confidence. Listen to me. You're solid, dependable, and if you tell him you're me, he'll believe you.'' As if rolling her own words over in her head, Theresa quickly added, ''If you do something with your hair besides run your fingers through it and put on something decent, you could carry it off. You know you could.'' It wasn't the first time they had pretended to be each other, although the last time had been years ago. ''We do have the same bone structure, even though mine is a little finer.''

The additional comment was pure Theresa, so pure that T.J. merely shook her head at the evaluation. Theresa didn't mean anything by it. As children, they had been almost carbon copies of each other. But while Theresa had devoted herself to zealously enhancing what nature had so bountifully granted in the first place, T.J. had shrugged it off and concentrated on her studies and being her father's daughter.

That meant vanity never entered into the picture. Shawn Cochran had a selflessness that bordered on religious fervor. He had long ago detached himself from the family firm, leaving it to his younger brother to develop. Instead, Shawn had devoted himself to whatever cause needed him the most at the moment. It was T.J.'s mother who had supported the family. Responsibility and hard work had been a part of T.J.'s life for as long as she could remember. That didn't leave much time for being carefree and frivolous.

Or spending hours looking into a mirror, perfecting the perfect pout.

Theresa took care of that in spades.

Like her father before her, Theresa knew just how to hire and retain good people who in turn made her look good. She rewarded them well and expected a great deal in return. Her cousin was no exception.

Theresa's father, Philip, had seen T.J.'s creative talents early on and, in his own no-nonsense way, had decided to nurture them. Accepting no excuses from his sister-in-law or his niece, he sent T.J. to Harvard when T.J.'s parents had had barely enough money to send her to a community college.

Upon graduation, T.J. had come to work for the family firm out of gratitude, loyalty and a need to create. She had been at it for seven years now and she loved her work as well as her cousin. But this was asking for something above and beyond the call of duty.

And T.J. had a bad feeling about it. "I'd rather you played you. After all, you're better at it."

"You're not giving yourself enough credit," Theresa insisted. "Remember high school?"

The feeling of déjà vu turned icy.

"When I took your SATs for you?"

"You saved my skin, then."

That was because they hadn't been caught. But

they easily could have been. "It could have very well been both our necks," she reminded Theresa.

T.J. still hated thinking of that. It had been a stupid thing to do, risking both their futures, but Theresa had come to her in tears, completely unprepared for the test that T.J. had taken the month before. Theresa had been terrified of not doing well and bringing down her father's wrath on her head.

Moved, T.J. had gone in for Theresa. Shaking inwardly, she had managed to fool everyone and take the test. She had scored high enough for her cousin for Philip Cochran to reward Theresa with a keepsake diamond.

The diamond was the first of many she was to go on to collect.

This time, though, there was a very simple solution before them and T.J. couldn't understand why Theresa was missing it. "Look, Theresa, it's not like you're deliberately standing him up to go skiing. Why don't we just tell him the truth? That you were in an accident and are being held hostage against your will by a muscular doctor. I can't see MacAffee not being reasonable about it. We could reschedule—"

"Can't." The single word cut T.J. short. "This was the only pocket of time he had available that I could accommodate. Besides, if we reschedule, he might just decide to go with that other company that's been courting him. Whitney and Son." Theresa fairly spat out the name of their number-one competitor. "C'mon, T.J. You could do it again. MacAffee is coming by just to give me the once-over. You're probably more his type than I am." Theresa meant it without malice, unaware of the way the appraisal hurt. "You know, serious."

Defensively, T.J. slipped on the oversize glasses she used for reading and went back to work on her computer. "Stuffy."

Theresa glossed over the wounded tone, only vaguely hearing it. There wasn't much time. "You said it, I didn't."

T.J. knew Theresa was waiting for an answer. "I'd really rather not, Theresa."

Theresa wasn't prepared for any opposition. Taking her by surprise, it left her speechless for exactly half a second. Then she rallied.

"Please?" Like a train leaving the station, Theresa's voice took on momentum as she spoke. "It'd only be for a few hours. Show him the rest of the campaign you've been working on. He really liked the preliminary drawings we sent up."

It was a royal "we" and T.J. was used to it. She had been the one who had worked on the preliminary drawings, faxing them up to MacAffee Toys' headquarters in San Jose as she went along.

T.J. felt herself weakening. Not that she really wanted to pretend to be Theresa, but in her recollection, she had never actually said no to her cousin.

"Theresa, I—"

Theresa heard what she wanted in T.J.'s tone. "Done. Well, I'm going to see if I can get that doctor to give me a sponge bath—"

Her screen saver came on, a little mouse running madly in a wheel to keep from slipping and being rattled around. T.J. knew exactly how the mouse felt. She hit a key and the tiny cartoon rodent disappeared.

"Doctors don't give sponge baths, Theresa. They have the nurses do that."

The chuckle was deep, throaty and entirely sensual. "Always a first time. Give me a call later. I'm at Harris Memorial. Room 312. Bye."

Like a leaf falling to the ground in the aftermath of a whirlwind, T.J. felt dizzy.

"Wait! When is he supposed to be here?" In typical Theresa fashion, Theresa was leaving her without any details, depending on the fact that she could ferret them out herself.

T.J. wasn't in the mood to ferret.

Theresa hadn't quite hung up. "Eleven o'clock. He's arriving from San Jose at LAX. American Airways. Flight 17. Emmett is going with the limo to pick him up. Might be nice if you were in it," she added.

"Be nicer if you were in it." But T.J. was talking to a dial tone. She sighed, replacing the receiver. Eleven o'clock. That didn't give her much time.

Heidi Wallace, Theresa's executive secretary, peeked into T.J.'s office less than a minute later. An understanding smile swept over the woman's finely lined face as she walked in. She laid a black garment bag over the back of the only other chair in the office.

"Swept right over you, didn't she?"

T.J. looked down at herself before glancing back at the other woman. "Do the tread marks show that much?"

Heidi laughed. A sense of humor was a prerequisite for working with Theresa Cochran.

"Wide and deep."

T.J. sighed, unconsciously eyeing the garment bag. "How did you know?"

"She called me first." Heidi was already heading for the door. "Emmett will be around to pick you up in the limo at ten-thirty." T.J.'s brows rose in surprise. "Seems she didn't think you would say no."

And why should she? I never have so far. "I suppose there's no harm in it."

Turning her swivel chair so that she faced the windows, T.J. looked at her reflection in the glass. With a resigned sigh, she held her hair away from her neck. Maybe if she wore it up...

Heidi could see half a dozen ways it could cause harm, but she wasn't being paid to comment on that. "If you say so. But if you're going to take La Cochran's place, I'd say you need a bit of a quick makeover." She nodded toward the bag Theresa had instructed her to bring to T.J. Inside was one of her business suits, complete with matching shoes and purse.

T.J. was dressed more casually than usual, having slipped on jeans and a baggy pullover before leaving home this morning. Theresa had never cared what she wore as long as she held up her end of the load. T.J. pointedly ignored the garment bag.

"Christopher MacAffee is coming to talk business. I don't think he's going to care what I look like as long as the campaign is conducted with dignity and profit."

Heidi had her instructions. "Humor me—and her. The head of C & C Advertising shouldn't look as if she was taking in laundry on the side." Heidi picked up the garment bag and laid it across T.J.'s desk.

"She keeps a change of clothing in the office in case she's, um, working all night."

Or entertaining a client, T.J. thought.

"Why don't you make use of it?" Heidi prodded.

T.J. pushed herself away from her desk and rose to her feet, eyeing the bag. "She really was sure of me, wasn't she?"

Heidi crossed her arms before her. T.J.'s easygoing disposition was a matter of record. "When have you ever given her cause for doubt?"

T.J. didn't answer. Instead, she took the garment bag and went to Theresa's suite of offices to change.

Okay, so how bad could it be?

EMMETT MITCHELL, C & C Advertising's chauffeur for the last three decades, held up a large placard with Christopher MacAffee's name on it. He aimed it at the sea of people disembarking from the airplane that stood tethered to the side of the building by means of a carpeted corridor.

Beside him, T.J. shifted uncomfortably in Theresa's high heels, scanning the crowd. She had never met Christopher MacAffee, but she knew that he was a tall, stately-looking man with dark hair and a demeanor that would have easily placed him at the head of a Victorian household a hundred years ago.

Her eyes flickered briefly over the tall, dark-haired man who was just emerging from the plane in the distance. He was the kind of man Theresa would pounce on with relish, T.J. thought. Her own pulse scrambled a little as she watched him walk toward her.

Of course he was walking toward her, she thought

disparagingly. Everyone on the plane was walking toward her. She was in the direct path of the disembarking passengers.

T.J. glanced at the chauffeur on her left. Emmett looked like a gnarled gnome, his skin a leather brown that seemed to complement the light beige livery he wore. "Do you see him anywhere, Emmett?"

In response, the snowy-haired man who had once driven her uncle and her grandfather before him shook his head firmly.

"Can't say I do, miss." He raised the placard higher with a touch of impatience. "But I haven't the faintest idea who I'm looking for to begin with."

"That makes two of us." She sighed. "It would have been easier on us if his father was still president. I once saw a photo of him in a magazine—a tall, thin man in his mid-sixties."

"Oh, a young guy."

T.J. struggled to hide her smile. Emmett had changed his mind about his age several times in the past fifteen years, fearing retirement would be forced on him. He pushed the number back periodically.

"Yes, like you," she agreed.

That drop-dead-gorgeous-looking man in the gray Armani suit was still coming toward her, T.J. noted out of the corner of her eye. As she turned her head, he made eye contact with her.

Her pulse jumped as Mr. Gorgeous stopped right in front of her.

The man nodded at the placard in Emmett's hands. "I believe you're looking for me."

The words *All of my life* materialized on her lips and it took effort to actually keep from saying them.

Instead, she heard herself saying, "You're not Christopher MacAffee."

He smiled and T.J.'s blood warmed several degrees, turning the cold airport lobby almost balmy. "Why wouldn't I be?"

"No reason." *Smooth, T.J., smooth.*

The grin widened, showing off teeth that rivaled Theresa's precious snow-capped mountains. "I'm happy to hear that, because I am." He put out his hand to her. "Christopher MacAffee."

It took her a second to assimilate the information. Belatedly, T.J. put out her own hand and shook his. Christopher's grip was firm and warm. She felt something twist within her stomach and knot.

"And I'm—" *Tongue-tied.*

"Theresa Cochran," Christopher finished for her. Eyes the color of sunlight-warmed grass bathed her in their light as he smiled at her. "I'd recognize you anywhere, although I have to say you're even better looking in person than you are on the society page."

"There's a reason for that," Emmett muttered under his breath as he lowered the placard to his side.

T.J. shot him a silencing look. They had gone over the charade and the need for it during the ride to the airport. She knew exactly what Emmett thought of it. Not much, but winning the account would be a prestigious feather in their cap.

Emmett chuckled.

In an attempt to draw Christopher's attention away from what would cause her chauffeur to chuckle like that, T.J. spoke quickly, though her voice sounded a little squeaky to her ear at first. "Thank you, Mr. MacAffee. Why don't you just follow me?"

With a slight inclination of his head, Christopher linked his arm through T.J.'s. "With the utmost of pleasure. And it's Christopher, please."

"Christopher, please what?" T.J. heard herself asking. Oh, Lord, she was flirting, just like Theresa. It had to be the suit.

He laughed then, a deep throaty laugh that curled through her like hickory smoke, warm and scented. "They were right about you," he murmured as he took out his handkerchief and dabbed at the fresh perspiration on his forehead. "You really are something else."

Her heart skipped a beat, even though she knew that the compliment was meant for Theresa and whatever preconceived notions she must have conjured up in Christopher's mind.

"You don't know the half of it," she replied with what she hoped was a sexy smile.

2

THE PALM THAT GRIPPED the hand rest on the escalator undulating its way down to the ground floor of the airport was clammy and Christopher was very aware of it. He was also acutely aware that the world around him was spinning ever so slightly if he didn't concentrate on hanging on to it with both hands.

Christopher refused to give in to the feeling that had accompanied him all during the flight and threatened to overwhelm him now. He didn't have time to be sick.

Instead, he forced himself to concentrate on the reason he was here in this overcrowded, stuffy airport. His brain felt as if there were a fog descending upon it. He was halfway through the electronic doors before he remembered. Christopher stopped abruptly. It took him a moment to focus on the woman next to him.

"What?" T.J. turned luminous blue eyes up at his face. Was it her imagination, or did he look a little pale?

"I forgot. I brought a valise with me. It should be coming onto the luggage carousel by now." Wherever that was, he thought. Disorientation mushroomed.

Reluctantly, T.J. backtracked into the airport lobby, her arm still hooked through Christopher's. She had the impression she was steadying him. "Oh, I didn't know you were staying overnight."

Damn, wasn't it just like Theresa to neglect to fill her in on the details? Just how long was she supposed to keep up this charade, anyway?

Christopher blinked to clear his vision, but his eyes still felt moist and watery. And a tremendous pounding had begun in his temples. Terrific way to conduct business.

"I'm not." Moving on leaden legs, Christopher found a place by the carousel. Luggage from two flights comingled on the conveyor belt as their owners stood around the perimeter, trying to spot individual pieces.

He'd gone to meet with his father yesterday. The old man was just getting over an intense twenty-four-hour case of the flu. He'd spent more than half the visit going on about it. Christopher was getting the uneasy feeling that perhaps advice hadn't been the only thing the older man had given him.

"I brought along some of our latest toys so that whoever is assigned to the account could get a feeling for them if and when I sign."

If and when. The man knew how to keep people on their toes. T.J. nodded. "That would be me."

He narrowed his brows. It took more effort than he would have thought. "You work on the account directly?"

That was a slip. Theresa never did, but maybe he didn't know that. *This isn't going to be easy,* she thought.

"Sometimes," T.J. amended quickly. She decided to embellish. How would he know the difference?

"When the account really interests me." And working on the proposals for MacAffee Toys had really fired her imagination. "I guess I've never outgrown my love for toys." She laughed quietly. A small woman elbowed a towering hulk of a man out of the way as she claimed three pieces of garish luggage. T.J. stepped aside. "Which makes playing with Megan very easy."

All the suitcases were beginning to look alike. He wondered uneasily if his had been lost.

"Megan?"

Just the sound of the little girl's name brought a fond smile to T.J.'s lips. Her marriage had been a mistake from the moment she and Peter had left the church, but Megan had been a wonderful consolation prize. Thirty pounds of trouble, energy and sticky fingers. "My daughter."

Christopher raised his eyes from the carousel. "You have a daughter?"

She wondered if he had brought anything that would capture Megan's imagination. "Yes," she murmured absently as she scanned the spinning collection of luggage. Why hadn't he just carried it on with him?

Christopher always liked to know who he was dealing with. Nothing in the background his people had presented him with mentioned that Theresa Cochran had ever been married or given birth to a child.

"I didn't know you had a daughter."

T.J. caught the warning look Emmett flashed her. Abruptly, her words replayed themselves in her head. Damn, she had to keep her mind off the way her heels pinched and on the fact that she was supposed to be

Theresa and not herself. Theresa had no children. She had never been married.

T.J.'s mouth twisted in a self-deprecating smile. And if it hadn't been for a really horrid eight months she would rather forget, neither had she. But the brief union had given her Megan and that had made all the difference in the world to her. Megan was worth enduring anything.

She ignored Emmett's knowing look and stared straight ahead at the luggage carousel, willing the valise to materialize.

"I'm sorry. I love her so much that sometimes I forget she really isn't mine." She could feel both Christopher and Emmett looking at her. Emmett, no doubt, was dying to see just how she intended to pull herself out of this. "She's my cousin's two-year-old. T.J. knows how crazy I am about her and right now, she's letting me play Mom. I have her for the weekend."

Mentally biting her lip, T.J. forced herself to calm down and take it slow. People, after all, saw what they thought they saw. And Christopher thought he was seeing Theresa. That made things a little easier for her. She just had to perpetuate that impression—and stop tripping over her own tongue.

She smiled, letting the expression drift sensually over her face and eyes the way she had seen Theresa do so many times.

"At times I really do feel as if she were my own. Megan's a terrific little girl." As an addendum, T.J. grabbed onto the first thing that occurred to her. "My cousin is away on a skiing trip."

"Skiing." How long had it been since he had allowed himself to get away for a skiing trip? He couldn't remember. "That sounds like fun."

The idea of standing on two skinny boards while sailing down a mountainside slick with snow did not come under her definition of fun.

"So they say."

Christopher looked down at T.J. quizzically. She made it sound as if she didn't care for it. "'They?'" he echoed. "Funny, I thought I read somewhere that you were an avid skier."

Dummy. You've got to stop answering as you. Theresa loved to ski. "I am," she said quickly. She let another rosy smile curve her mouth. "I was just being flippant. They tell me I do that a lot."

He looked as if he bought it, she thought. T.J could feel her heart fluttering madly. She was way out of practice. There had been a time where a simple switch would have been a challenge to her, not an obstacle course to overcome. Frazzled nerves insisted on knitting together, causing more unrest inside her.

"Do you ski?" she asked, turning the conversation away from "herself" and onto safer ground. *Damn it, Theresa, why did you have to pick today to get into an accident?*

"I used to." For a moment, an isolated scene from his past rose in his mind's eye. College. Winter break. And powdered snow so pure, it looked as if it belonged in a Currier and Ives painting. "Maybe we could get together sometime and test the powder at Vail."

This was probably the nineties equivalent of "We'll do lunch sometime," she mused.

"Maybe," T.J. agreed slyly, giving him her best

Theresa imitation. She glanced back toward the carousel. A large black valise was just being belched out onto the conveyor belt. Mentally, she crossed her fingers. "Is that your suitcase?"

It took him a moment to recognize it. "Yes, that's mine." Christopher reached for it just as a sharp abdominal pain cut his breath away.

When Christopher hesitated, Emmett closed his fingers round the handle. "Nice save," the chauffeur murmured to T.J.

T.J. lowered her voice. She knew he was referring to her lapse about skiing. "Glad someone is enjoying themselves."

"Best time I've had in years," the old man said with a chuckle. Thin, sinewy arms strained beneath the livery as he hefted the suitcase off the carousel.

Emmett had all but raised the Cochran girls in the limousine and although Theresa was now his boss, he was partial to T.J. They all were. T.J. had grown up to be one of them, without any airs or pretentiousness. Theresa, pampered, spoiled, accustomed to being obeyed, always behaved—perhaps without even meaning to—as if she was a cut above the people who worked for her.

They had no choice but to forgive her, but the line that divided her from them was always there.

There was no such line with T.J., despite the fact that she and Theresa shared the same company-founding grandfather. Its absence bred the strong bond of loyalty T.J. inspired.

Christopher moved to take the valise from the old man. Chauffeur or not, it didn't seem right that the man should have to struggle with the luggage.

His strength failed him.

Christopher had told himself it was because he hadn't taken the time to eat anything this morning. Never a fussy eater, he usually enjoyed almost everything he sampled. This time around, however, he'd skipped breakfast. And the food on the plane had been completely unappetizing to him. Even the sight of it being passed out to other passengers had caused his stomach to lurch in protest.

Just as it was doing now. The cold sweat that accompanied it wasn't welcomed, either.

He was turning as gray as his suit. T.J. took Christopher's arm, suddenly envisioning him passing out at her feet. ''Anything wrong?''

Christopher shook his head, which was a mistake. Dizziness descended over him, bringing with it little pointy spears that jabbed him from all sides.

T.J. braced her shoulder against Christopher just as he sagged.

He flashed what he hoped was an apologetic smile, struggling to straighten. It took effort for him to do both. ''I'm not sure.''

Perspiration was now popping out all along a very handsome brow. This wasn't good.

''Emmett,'' T.J. called to the back of the man's head.

Shifting the weight of the valise to his other hand, Emmett turned. Concern slithered over his bony face. He left the valise behind him as he hurried over. ''What happened?''

Christopher felt like a fool. He also felt weak. Weaker than he could ever remember feeling in his life.

"I don't know. Suddenly I feel as if I have tissues for knees." He looked at T.J., who had propped herself under his arm. Any other time, he would have enjoyed having such a beautiful woman so close to him. Now, even the light delicate scent he detected on her hair was making him dizzy. He tried to raise another apologetic smile and had no idea if he succeeded. "Must be the company."

"Yeah, I have that effect on men." The quip was equal parts sarcastic and self-deprecating. The last time anyone had said she'd made him weak in the knees, it was because she had hit him from behind. She'd been eight at the time.

"But not this bad," she realized. Mothering instincts took over and T.J. felt Christopher's brow. It was damp and feverish to the touch. "You're hot," she said with dismay.

"I've been told that," Christopher mumbled, or thought he did. It was an effort to keep from being swallowed up by the lightheadedness that was reaching out for him.

Nervousness faded. What she had on her hands was a situation and T.J. was never better than when she was handling problems. It was a hell of a lot easier dealing with a crisis than it was pretending to be someone else, even if it was Theresa.

"Emmett, help me get him to the limo." As the smaller man lent his support on Christopher's other side, T.J. caught the attention of a passing attendant. She commandeered him into service. "I need help with this man's valise."

Picking it up, the man followed them out to the loading zone.

Five minutes later, with the attendant's help, T.J. got Christopher into the back seat of the limousine. Pressing a tip into the man's hand, T.J. climbed in beside a rapidly worsening Christopher.

Even before the limo left the curb, T.J. got to work. She loosened Christopher's tie quickly. The shirt beneath his jacket was wringing wet and plastered to a surprisingly muscular chest.

Christopher was vaguely aware of the fluttering, light fingers working over him. He didn't like not being in control and he hated being ill, which was exactly what, to his enfeebled disgust, he was. Out of control and sick as a dog.

He tried for flippancy when all else seemed to be eluding him, escaping like mice leaving a sinking ship. He laid one hand over hers, stilling her fingers. "Why, Ms. Cochran, we hardly know each other."

She wondered if deep down, there was a Southerner mixed in with his ancestry. The man oozed charm even as he perspired. "I don't have to know you well to loosen your tie. You're sick, Mr. MacAffee."

Tell me something I don't know. "Beautiful, intelligent and clairvoyant, too, what more could a person ask for?"

How she wished Theresa was here to handle this. "A lot of things."

Emmett glanced over his shoulder. The limo was in the far lane, the one that ultimately wound up threading into the freeway. He needed a destination before then. "Where to?"

Christopher had the most beautiful dark lashes, T.J. thought, looking at the man's pale face. Lashes that any woman would have killed to have. Right now, they fluttered along a very pale cheek. Emmett cleared his throat dramatically. Caught, she flushed, her eyes shifting to the chauffeur.

"What?"

"Where do you want me to drive?" Emmett nodded toward Christopher. Slumped in his seat, Christopher looked as if he was only semiconscious. "You don't want to take him to the office like this, do you?"

"No." T.J. bit her lip. She bent over closer to Christopher. "Do you want to go to the hospital?"

There were two of her now. He tried to pick out which one was the real Theresa. He chose the one on the left. "No, this is exactly what the old man had. It'll pass in twenty-four hours." Although, right now, it felt as if he was going to pass with it.

"A virus with a wristwatch," T.J. muttered under her breath with a shake of her head. Now what? She blew out a long breath as Christopher's head drooped onto her shoulder. "Well, you're in no condition to fly home or to go to the office." She looked at Emmett. "Maybe we'd better book him into a hotel."

Emmett snorted. "Good luck with that."

"What do you mean?" He was obviously privy to something she didn't know. The last thing she was in the mood for was games.

"Haven't you heard? There's a computer convention in town. It's so big, they had to split it in half. One half's at the Anaheim Convention Center, the other's in L.A. There're computer nerds spread out all over the place and probably not a single thing left except a manger behind the inn."

She blew out a breath. "Great."

Christopher looked as if he were unconscious. There was no other choice available to her. Besides, she really didn't like the idea of just dumping him in some suite, no matter how high priced. After all, the man was sick. It wouldn't be right to leave him alone.

T.J. made up her mind. "Take him to my house, Emmett."

Emmett's tufted brows disappeared beneath the brim of his cap as he turned to look at her. "Your place?" His expression was dubious. "Are you sure?"

"I'm sure," she answered, resigned.

"NO, I CAN WALK," Christopher protested when Emmett tried to brace himself on one side of him. T.J. was holding him up on the other.

The protest died as Christopher sagged between them. They both made a grab for him, barely succeeding in keeping his knees and his very sharply pressed crease from making contact with the driveway.

"Maybe tomorrow," T.J. promised. "You can walk all you want tomorrow." *In fact, I'll insist on it.*

There were no more words of protest. "You make a nice crutch."

T.J. shifted to get a better position beneath his outstretched arm. She held on to his hand for balance. "I'll include that in my résumé."

He looked at her, or tried to. He was beginning to feel mildly giddy. "Do presidents of family-owned companies need résumés?"

She thought of her father, who would have been president if only his sense of moral duty hadn't taken him into parts unknown. "Sometimes."

"I'll have to keep that in mind," Christopher mumbled. He blinked, trying to focus on the two-story house before him. He vaguely wondered if it was real, or, like the two images of Theresa in the limo, this was an illusion, too. "This isn't what I expected."

T.J. thought of Theresa's large, rambling three-story structure in Beverly Hills. It was as homey as a museum and often reminded her of one. Had Christopher seen a photo of it somewhere? T.J. seemed to vaguely recall that Theresa had opened the estate up to a film crew from a popular tabloid program a year or so ago.

"I like to live unpretentiously," she answered crisply, hoping that would put an end to his questions for now.

Whatever else Christopher was about to say in response, he didn't. Instead, the front walk seemed to come spinning up at him. When he closed his eyes to avoid the sight of the pending impact, he found himself wrapped up completely in darkness.

T.J. felt the difference immediately. She almost tumbled backward as all one hundred and eighty pounds of Christopher MacAffee turned into deadweight. "Oh my God. Emmett!"

"I have him," the older man cried with more confidence than he exhibited. His voice was strained as he struggled to keep from sinking to his knees beneath the weight. Emmett couldn't even move his head to look at T.J. "I'm asking for a raise after this."

T.J. gritted her teeth. Between the two of them,

they managed to keep Christopher upright. "I'll put in a recommendation."

She pressed the doorbell urgently, hoping that Cecilia hadn't taken Megan out somewhere for the afternoon. There were house keys in her purse, but T.J. was afraid that any sudden move to initiate a search would throw them all off balance.

"C'mon, c'mon, Cecilia, open the door." T.J. leaned on the bell.

A moment later, T.J.'s housekeeper threw open the door. Bewilderment transformed into amazement, and then satisfaction, all in the blink of an eye.

The six-foot-four woman grinned at T.J. as she got out of the way. "You brought home a man."

"Don't get excited, Cecilia. We can't keep him. He's only on loan from Theresa." Was it her imagination, or was Christopher getting heavier with each step?

Dark gray eyes did a quick appraisal. The grin broadened. "I do like the cut of the lady's castoffs." Cecilia peered at Christopher more closely. It wasn't her imagination. The man *was* unconscious. "What's the matter with him?"

"He's sick." T.J. huffed out the words. Perspiration was sliding down the small of her back. "This way, Emmett." She inclined her head toward the right. "We'll put him in my room."

"I'll flip you for him," Cecilia said with a deep, throaty laugh, leading the way to T.J.'s bedroom.

Their path was suddenly blocked by an animated little girl. Her honey brown hair fluttered all around her head like a fluffy halo, giving her a cherubic look that camouflaged a mischievous streak.

With an elated cry, Megan dropped the action figures she had been playing with and hurried forward, about to throw herself into her mother's arms.

T.J. snapped to attention. "Catch the flying daughter" was a game she couldn't play today. The last thing she wanted was to expose Megan to whatever it was that had struck down Christopher.

"Cecilia, quick, take Megan to the family room. I don't want her coming in contact with Christopher."

Cecilia caught Megan by the edge of her rompers and scooped her up. Holding on to thirty pounds of wiggling child was a challenge. She bounced the little girl against her hip.

"Don't blame you." She grinned as she retreated. "If I had a man like that leaning all over me, I wouldn't want to share him, either."

T.J. was in no mood for Cecilia's sense of humor. "Because he's sick, Cecilia, because he's sick. And he's not mine. He's a client."

Cecilia paused in the hall to give Christopher a long, last appraising look. "I'd say that business seems to be looking up."

The woman was impossible. Not even her own mother, with her prim sense of decorum and traditional roles, had been this bad. Ever since she had hired Cecilia to help care for Megan, the older woman had appointed herself T.J.'s personal matchmaker. T.J. wanted no matches. All she wanted out of life was to do her work and devote her spare time to Megan. That was enough happiness, she thought, for any person.

"He certainly is a big guy." Emmett was visibly

struggling as they brought Christopher across the threshold and into the bedroom.

"Just be glad my bedroom's not on the second floor." The bed had never looked so far away from the door.

"So what are you going to do with him?" Emmett puffed as they deposited Christopher's inert body onto the bed.

Waiting until her own breathing leveled out before answering, T.J. took Christopher's shoes off and placed them beside her bed.

He looked completely out of place here in her room, in her bed.

Like some fantasy come true, she couldn't help thinking. If her fantasies ran in that direction. Which they didn't. Marriage to Peter had taken care of that for her.

T.J. shrugged in answer to Emmett's question as she raked her fingers through her wayward hair. "Undress him, I guess."

"Oh, please, let me do it," Cecilia called from the next room.

Despite everything, T.J. laughed. "You get to undress the next sick man I drag in. Besides, one of us exposed to this twenty-four-hour virus of his or whatever he has is enough."

Reaching for Christopher's jacket, she stopped. The idea of even partially undressing Christopher was suddenly far too personal, virus or no virus.

T.J. looked at Emmett. "No, wait. You undress him and I'll go to the supermarket and get some orange juice and aspirin."

Megan was safely planted in front of an elaborate

fort Cecilia had constructed for her earlier. That meant she had bought them about five minutes. Using it, Cecilia ventured back into the narrow hall, eyeing the man in T.J.'s bed.

"You're passing up a chance like that?" There was no way she would have let modesty dictate her actions if she had the choice.

This was getting old. "Cecilia, he's a client. Which reminds me, don't call me T.J. around him."

This had come out of left field. "Why? What should I call you?"

T.J. frowned. "Theresa." She had been T.J. ever since Theresa had been born. It had been an incredible sense of competition that had prompted Philip Cochran to mimic his brother and name his firstborn and, subsequently, only daughter after their mother.

Cecilia's small eyes became even smaller as she narrowed them. "I thought you hated being called that."

She shrugged. "I do, but he—" she nodded toward Christopher "—doesn't know I'm me."

Cecilia watched as Emmett peeled Christopher's shirt away and sucked in her breath at the sight of the almost perfect torso. "He passed out on your shoulder and he doesn't know who you are?"

T.J. didn't feel like getting into it now. "It's complicated." Cecilia obviously wasn't budging without some sort of an explanation. T.J. gave it grudgingly. "Theresa was supposed to meet with him, but she got into a car accident. She's okay," she said quickly before Cecilia could ask, "but they want to keep her in the hospital overnight for observation just in case. Christopher heads MacAffee Toys and only wants to deal with the head man, or woman in this case. Which would be Theresa.''

Cecilia was trying to keep up. ''Who is in the hospital.''

Emmett, T.J. noted, was really struggling now. Christopher was much too large for him for manage. ''Now you're getting it.''

Cecilia put her hand to her forehead. ''What I'm getting is a headache.''

''You can have some of the aspirin when I get back.''

Exhausted, the chauffeur looked toward the two women. ''I need some help here.''

As Cecilia went to oblige, T.J. placed her hand on the woman's arm. ''I think you should avoid contact with him. Megan, remember?''

The wide lips split into a fresh grin. She gestured toward the bedroom. ''Be my guest.''

T.J. heard the older woman laughing to herself as she went back to the family room and Megan.

Squaring her shoulders, T.J. marched back into her bedroom.

You owe me for this, Theresa. Big-time.

3

CHRISTOPHER MACAFFEE couldn't remember a day in his life when he wasn't in control of a situation, when he was not *expected* to be in control of a situation. His father had been a stickler for discipline and decorum. His mother hadn't been there to temper the senior MacAffee. She'd divorced his father and left his life almost before he could form a clear memory of her.

A parade of solemn-eyed nannies with a clear-cut sense of what he was expected to do had marched through his formative years, teaching him by word and by example what sort of behavior was expected of him. And he was expected to always, always, be in control. Of his emotions, of his destiny, of basically pretty much everything.

That meant, among other things, being aware of where his pants were and where he was at any given moment in his life.

Christopher was aware of neither when he finally opened his eyes again.

The unfamiliar feel of satin greeted him along parts of his body that had never had firsthand acquaintance with the material. Sliding a hand beneath the covers informed him of two things: that he didn't have his pants on and that he was wearing what felt like a dress.

That alone startled him into complete wakefulness, a condition the rest of his body protested with feeling. The room he opened his eyes to was completely unfamiliar to him. That wasn't something he was unaccustomed to. He traveled a lot.

But there were subtle, female touches here and there—soft, filmy curtains billowing at the window, for instance, and a white eyelet comforter, which led him to believe that he wasn't in a hotel room.

The sound of childish laughter wafted from another room, like a tiny silver bell being rung in three-quarter time.

He was in someone's home.

Whose?

Christopher tried gathering his thoughts together and it was like trying to pick up peas that were being scattered from an overturned colander. The more he grasped at them, the more they rolled away from him. He tried again.

The last thing he remembered was sagging against a very soft shoulder. Cochran's. Then this was her house? He attempted to focus his mind.

Slowly, from behind a hazy curtain, fragments of a memory returned. A modest two-story house. A tremendously long walk from the door to…

Where?

Try as he might, Christopher couldn't remember where the walk ended. Probably here, which was why he didn't recall the room.

Digging palms into the mattress on either side of him, Christopher tried to sit up. A thousand disembodied hammers simultaneously began whacking away at his joints. The groan was involuntary and as much of a surprise as the sudden pain was.

Damn, he felt weak. Training had him struggling against the feeling and denying its very existence. He didn't have time for this.

The door to his room opened almost immediately in response to the groan. The woman he'd met at the airport stuck her head in.

Cochran.

Theresa, he thought, putting a first name to her. She looked concerned. Vaguely, he wondered why.

T.J. had just been about to enter her unexpected guest's room when she'd heard him groan. Her haste to open the door had almost made her drop the pitcher of orange juice she was carrying on a tray.

Recovering, she made it inside with glassware intact. T.J. peered at Christopher's face. He still looked pale, although it wasn't easy to detect at first. The man's olive complexion tended to make him look healthy. The sheen of perspiration along his hairline along with the cast of his eyes negated that.

Maybe she should have taken him to the hospital. It still wasn't too late. Emmett was killing time in the kitchen, just in case. He'd been there for the past five hours. Their guest had been sleeping that long.

T.J. eased the tray onto the nightstand. "How are you feeling?"

Like hell on a bad day, but he wasn't about to admit that. "Where are my pants?"

His voice was gruff. Maybe he wasn't as sick as she thought.

T.J. nodded toward the mirrored wardrobe. "In the

closet.'' The expensive trousers were better off on a hanger than wrinkling beneath her comforter. ''I thought you'd be more comfortable without them.''

Had she undressed him? he wondered. ''Only when I'm showering.''

T.J. shrugged. ''Suit yourself.''

Taking the gray trousers out of the closet, she deposited them at the foot of the bed, then smiled at him. Actually, it was hard not to laugh out loud. He wasn't the type to wear a dark blue, flowing nightshirt with flair.

''There, you can make good your escape anytime you want, although I wouldn't suggest going just yet.'' Crossing to him, she touched her palm to Christopher's forehead. It only confirmed what she already knew. ''You're still very warm, but then, it's only been a few hours.''

There might be a sickly cast to his eyes, but they were still far too green for her comfort. T.J. looked away. Picking the pitcher up, she filled his glass up halfway.

''I brought you some orange juice.'' She offered the glass to him. ''You need plenty of fluids to flush out your fever.''

Her touch had been soft, light. It stirred something distant within him. Something that responded to the concern he saw in her eyes.

Just went to show you couldn't believe everything you read. His report on Theresa Cochran had her pegged as a social butterfly, more interested in making temperatures rise than in lowering them.

Apparently, she was capable of both.

"A few hours?" he echoed, suddenly registering what she'd said earlier.

She nodded. "Five. You've been asleep."

"I have a flight," he began weakly. What time was it, anyway?

"I already took care of that." She'd gone through his pockets to find the return ticket. "You're booked on a flight for Sunday." Two days should do it, she thought. If he got well faster, they could always reschedule again. "And I called your assistant to tell him what happened."

All he could do was nod weakly and let things happen. "Very efficient," he managed.

"We try to please. Now drink."

After a beat, he finally took the glass from her. "Is this your house?"

"Yes." T.J. looked pointedly at the glass.

He didn't care for orange juice, but because she'd gone to the trouble of getting it for him, he drank. There was something about her that told him she would press the issue if he refused. He wasn't up to carrying on a debate.

The juice stung his throat. "Why did you bring me here?"

She lifted a shoulder casually and resisted the temptation of pushing a wayward lock of hair from his forehead. There had been enough touching. "You were sick. Tossing you out by the side of the road just didn't seem right."

Flippant. Flippant usually irritated him. He found it vaguely amusing this time and didn't have the energy to question it. "Why not a hotel?"

She could have sworn he was challenging her. It

made her wonder how he would have treated her if the tables had been turned.

"There's a huge computer convention in town. The only room I could have gotten you was with a church mouse. Upper berth." An easy smile curved her mouth. "Besides, leaving a sick man in a hotel room by himself didn't seem quite right, either."

He tried to evaluate her motives. The hammering in his head made it difficult.

"Bad for business," he guessed. In his experience, people didn't go out of their way for one another unless they wanted something. There was no mystery here. He represented a lucrative contract for her company.

T.J. sighed inwardly. He was a cynic. Sad that someone so young and good-looking was so turned off by the world. But that, she reminded herself, was none of her business. Her job was to convince him that she was Theresa, get him to approve the contracts, then pack him up and send him on his way, nothing else.

How would Theresa have answered him? "Yes, that, too."

Dark brows drew together and furrowed over an almost perfect nose. "Too?"

She mimicked a smile she'd seen on Theresa's face countless times. Sexy, yet aloof enough to be intriguing. She looked at his wrist before answering. "I'm a pushover for a racing pulse and yours was."

T.J. took the glass from his hand and placed it on the tray, then very deliberately smoothed out the comforter. She leaned over so that her face was just inches from his. For a moment, she felt her own pulse scrambling, then dismissed it.

"Now get some rest," she ordered sweetly, "and we'll discuss business whenever you feel up to it."

Even in his slightly confused state, he could feel the woman fairly sizzled with sex. It went along with her reputation, but seemed almost incongruous with the jaunty ponytail that bobbed to and fro atop her head. She'd somehow managed to wrap a rubber band around the voluminous mass of hair he remembered earlier. For a split second, he entertained the thought of snapping that band and watching her hair come tumbling down again.

He wasn't really well yet, Christopher thought.

It didn't keep him from trying to get up. "I feel up to it now."

The hell he did. You only had to take one look at him to know he was pushing it. She placed a firm hand against his chest and forced him back down. It wasn't hard.

"All right, when *I* feel up to it," she amended. "I don't at the moment. Why don't you take the opportunity this lull provides and get some more rest?" she proposed sunnily.

He was being patronized. Christopher knew he should argue with her, but he suddenly felt too tired. Resigned, he supposed that no vast eternal plan would be altered if he waited a few hours before beginning this meeting that fate seemed determined to postpone.

With a sigh, he slid down against the pillows.

T.J. took it as a victory. Smiling, she retreated from the bed.

Christopher had never been aware of jeans looking quite that enticing before. He felt vaguely aroused.

"Theresa," he called after her.

Theresa. She was Theresa. Widening her smile, she turned at the door. Edginess buzzed in her brain. She hoped it didn't show.

"Yes?"

He had to know. Christopher picked at the dark blue nightshirt, holding it away from his chest. It was way too large to fit Theresa. It was almost too large for him. "Who does this belong to?"

T.J. grinned. She'd wondered when he'd get around to asking. "Cecilia, my housekeeper."

He was six-two. That meant she must have one hell of a housekeeper. "Oh, I thought perhaps it belonged to some former lover."

T.J. caught the tip of her tongue between her teeth. He had tactfully refrained from commenting on Cecilia's size. She rather liked that. Maybe he wasn't so brittle after all.

"I won't tell her you said that."

"Thanks."

He was asleep before he saw her close the door behind her.

THE SOUND OF LAUGHTER called to him, rousing Christopher and drawing him to the surface.

It intruded on his formless dream, pouring over it like sparkling golden honey, until it completely blotted out what had been before, substituting, instead, an incredible urge to join in the sound. To become one with it. Without the reserve his life had instilled on him, Christopher wanted it with every fiber of his being.

It was a child's laugh.

And yet it wasn't.

With effort, Christopher pried open his eyes and discovered to his relief that the room did not shimmer and swim before him when he raised his head. More than that, it remained still as he sat up.

Pleased, Christopher smiled as he took a deep breath. The queasiness he'd experienced earlier was still there, but on a scale of one to ten it had gone from a twelve to a two.

The laughter came again, surrounding him. Giggles. Little-girl giggles. He tried to concentrate. Hadn't the Cochran woman said something about a niece spending the weekend here?

A child. Christopher frowned slightly. It wasn't that he didn't like children; he just wasn't any good with them. Not the best thing to admit, he supposed, given the fact that the family fortune was built on an impish-faced doll called Moppsie that had found its way into thousands of homes more than sixty years ago. But he'd never gotten the knack of being at ease around children, even when he had been one himself.

It hadn't improved with age.

But the sound was inviting. Curiosity got the better of him.

The room tilted only slightly and then only for a moment as he reached to the edge of the bed for his trousers. He waited to get his bearings, then swung his legs over the side of the bed and got dressed. Partially. He had no idea where his shirt was and the uneasy feeling nagged at him that if he stopped to look for it, he would exhaust his supply of energy.

So, muttering under his breath, Christopher tucked in the long, flowing tails of the nightshirt into his pants. It took a lot of tucking. Christopher glanced down. It looked as if he was smuggling a spare tire. He looked absurd. Wearing the shirt out would have made him look even more ridiculous.

Opening the door, he let the sound of the laughter guide him. There were more giggles, accompanied by a deep, throaty laugh Christopher attributed to his hostess. Either that, he amended, or the housekeeper who probably moonlighted as a basketball player.

In either case, he wanted to see for himself. The laughter was coming from down the long hallway. He didn't bother closing the door behind him. Padding on the Spanish tile with bare feet, Christopher felt he was being led like one of the mice in *The Pied Piper of Hamelin.*

Might make for a good commercial, he thought, pleased with the image he'd conjured up.

He was even more pleased with what he saw when he reached what appeared to be the family room, because it fleshed out the sketchy image.

His hostess had forsaken her ponytail. The effect was akin to standing still for a one-two punch to the gut. Mechanically, he passed his hand over his abdomen.

Theresa, her hair partially tucked behind one ear, tumbling down on the other side, was kneeling on the floor beside an animated-looking little girl who could have been a magically enhanced miniature of the woman with her.

More giggles and squeals of pleasure ricocheted about the room, which was filled with toys. Theresa was entertaining her, speaking in a high voice and pretending to be the comical, stuffed royal lion she held in her hand. The lion was carrying on a discussion with a shorter, squatter-looking penguin. The latter had a lopsided crown on its head.

She was playing with the toys he'd brought down with him, Christopher realized. The annoyance that she'd taken it upon herself to go through his things faded in the wake of the pleasure the scene generated.

If it worked on him, it would certainly work on others, he decided.

Feeling as if he were privy to something that belonged in a video put out by a greeting-card company, Christopher leaned his shoulder against the doorjamb and watched in charmed silence.

T.J.'S BACK WAS to the doorway. Christopher had slept through the night. She'd gone in several times to check on him. Since he was still asleep this morning, T.J. had taken the time to play with her daughter. Having found the toys earlier in MacAffee's suitcase while she was rummaging for something more appropriate for him to wear during his convalescence, she'd decided to put them to good use.

Megan made a great audience.

T.J. twisted her hand from side to side, making the lion appear to be hopping from one foot to the other. His sorrowful expression almost seemed to change, reflecting the words she put into his mouth.

"Boy, oh boy, I wish I had a little girl to pull my string and help me talk. Talking is hard work." She turned the lion so that he faced the penguin. "Do you know where I can find a helpful little girl, Mr. Penguin?"

"King Penguin," the latter corrected indignantly, raising his head regally. Then he attempted to scratch his head, puzzled. The penguin shook his head haplessly. Both stuffed animals turned to Megan for help. "Do you know where we can find a helpful little girl?" the penguin asked her.

Megan's eyes shone with excitement. She jerked her thumb dead center into her chest. "Me," she cried. "Me. Me. Me."

The penguin nodded his head so hard, his crown fell over one eye. When he spoke, he had a definite Bronx accent. "Yes, you, you, you. Do you know where we can find a helpful little girl?"

Megan laughed, then narrowed her golden brown brows until they formed a V over her pert little nose. She placed her hands on the penguin, but knew better than to yank him away from her mother.

"Me, me liddle gurl."

Turning them so that they faced one another again, T.J. had the lion and the penguin exchange exaggerated looks, then jump as if the weight of a revelation had been physically dropped on them.

"She *is* a little girl," the lion said the way Sir Issac Newton might have once announced the discovery of gravity. King Penguin was appropriately speechless. Megan clapped her hands with glee. In unison, the stuffed animals presented their backs to Megan. "Do me?" the lion asked.

"No, *me,*" the penguin entreated. "Pull my string

first." The stuffed animal moved his royal butt adroitly and pushed the lion out of the way.

Holding her sides, Megan fell over on the floor, laughing at the show. The two stuffed animals promptly beset her on either side, cuddling, burrowing, adding to the source of her giggles.

If he could have found a way to bottle this, Christopher thought, he could make a fortune. Bottled happiness.

Megan's laughter was infectious. The more she heard it, the more T.J. laughed herself until both mother and daughter were rolling around on the floor like two children amid their toys.

"Man." Megan pointed a chubby finger abruptly toward the doorway.

T.J. looked and sucked in her breath when she saw Christopher standing there, watching them. *Yes, Bambi. Man has entered the forest.*

Christopher MacAffee looked a great deal taller when perceived from ground level on the rug. Embarrassed, T.J. quickly scrambled to her feet. She brushed her hands on the back of her jeans. They suddenly felt sweaty.

She cleared her throat, desperately wishing she had thought to close the door before entertaining Megan. "I'm sorry. Did we disturb you?"

The scene he'd happened on was so disarming, Christopher forgot that he felt awkward around anyone under four feet. Taking a step into the room, he couldn't take his eyes off the little girl. She looked like an exact copy of her aunt. Or the way he would have imagined she looked as a child.

If he were given to imagining things like that.

"If you mean did you wake me, yes. But I don't think you could call it being disturbed when the source of your merriment are two of the new toys I brought along."

"Oh, um, the suitcase." T.J. flushed like a child caught with her fingers in the cookie jar. He probably wasn't the type who would shrug off having his privacy invaded. She thought it was worth a shot. "I was really just looking to see if there was something a little bit more suitable for you to put on besides Cecilia's nightshirt." She bit her lip, then turned toward her daughter. Feeling herself on shaky ground, she decided to summon the cavalry. "Megan thinks your toys are great."

"So I see." Flanked on either side by the lion and the penguin, the little girl had a possessive arm wrapped around each. "Would you like to keep them, Megan?"

He had no idea what prompted him to give away the prototypes. It certainly wasn't like him. It just seemed like the thing to do at the time.

Megan looked up at the man who was as tall to her as some of the trees in the backyard. T.J. called the girl her little warrior. Megan was afraid of nothing. There was no hesitation in her response. Her head bobbed up and down as her eyes sparkled.

Maybe they could use the little girl in the commercial, he thought. "Then they're yours."

T.J. looked at him in surprise. A smile bloomed on her face. She hadn't had much time to be filled in on the new head of MacAffee Toys, but Heidi had given her a quick thumbnail sketch before she'd left for the airport yesterday. From what she was told, the man was efficient and all business. Never married, he had no children and had little tolerance for them.

Maybe they'd been wrong. He obviously knew how to get on the right side of a little girl.

T.J. laid a hand on his arm and brought his attention back to her. "That's very generous of you."

There was something about the look in her eyes that had him retreating. He wasn't sure from what, only that he needed to place some distance here.

The solemn expression changed his appearance entirely. It stripped him of his humanity. "They don't cost that much to produce. Besides, I presume you're going to want to keep them if we do wind up giving the account to you."

If. Well, that certainly took the shine off any thoughts she might have entertained about Mr. Christopher MacAffee and his generous nature.

"Yes," T.J. replied with just a touch of coolness, "we will." And then she saw Megan snuggle up against King Penguin. The ring of frost melted from T.J.'s heart. A good deed was a good deed, never mind about the ramifications. "Still, it's nice of you to let Megan handle the merchandise."

Christopher turned and then had to grab hold of the doorjamb to steady himself. Damn flu. "You did that before I had anything to say about it," he retorted with more gruffness than the situation warranted.

He was like a wounded bear. A cute, wounded bear in a blue nightshirt. The grin was spontaneous. "Don't you know how to accept a compliment graciously?"

"I thought I was."

Deftly she hooked her arm through his, determined to lead him back to the bed he had vacated.

"Maybe it's the fever." She touched his head. "You're cool." Now there was a surprise. Despite what Christopher had said at the airport, she figured he'd be ill for several days.

He could smell her hair. What was that? Jasmine? He would have thought someone in her position would have been wearing perfume that cost a few hundred dollars an ounce, not cologne. Still, it had a certain pleasing, arousing quality.

"Is that your medical opinion, or a social assessment?" he asked.

He was still a little shaky on his feet, she thought, and hoped that he wouldn't collapse the way he had yesterday. She glanced toward her room, then back at Megan. The little girl was busy with the stuffed animals.

"I don't know you socially." The words would have easily fit into Theresa's mouth, she congratulated herself. Theresa flirted whenever the opportunity presented itself.

He fell into the coy game effortlessly. "I'm told you know a lot of people socially."

Christopher saw a very formidable-looking woman emerging from another room. Taller than he, she made no attempt to disguise the fact that she was eyeing him. He was outnumbered.

This had to be the housekeeper, he thought. If anything, the nightshirt looked as if it might be too short for her.

Think Theresa, think Theresa. "I do," T.J. told him, "but you're not one of them. Yet." They were at her bedroom door. She coaxed him across the threshold. ''Now why don't you get back to bed and I'll bring around some chicken soup? I think you're up to eating that.''

He did still feel a little shaky. Suddenly the bed looked incredibly inviting. Only when he got into it did he look at the woman he thought was Theresa Cochran, thunderstruck. ''You're kidding, right?''

She grinned, relieved that he hadn't passed out before she'd gotten him into bed. ''I never kid when leading a man into my bedroom.''

There was no sense in fighting it. ''Any chance of some chicken in that chicken soup?''

''Every chance in the world,'' she promised with a smile, easing out of the room.

So far, she thought, *so good.*

4

THE FRAGRANCE that seemed woven into her hair surrounded him, replacing the very air as she bent over his bed to remove the tray she had brought in earlier. It was all Christopher could do not to reach out and touch the dark strands, to see if her hair was as soft as the scent of it led him to believe it was.

He fisted his hand around the sheet instead.

"It was good. The soup," he added when she turned her eyes up to his questioningly.

And it had been. So had the company. She'd remained in the room while he was eating, talking about trivial things that somehow seemed important when coming from her lips. And somewhere along the line, as she talked and he ate, he realized that he was feeling a great deal more human than he had just a little while ago.

He looked a little tense, T.J. thought. Well, that made two of them. Who would have thought that this charade would be so wearing on her? She didn't like lying; it always tangled things up.

Just like her stomach seemed to tangle up when he looked at her like that.

"We aim to please," T.J. answered as blithely as she could. She was about to whisk the tray away, but something kept her rooted to the spot. Deep, dark, green, the man's eyes were more potent than Super Glue.

Maybe it was the virus. He couldn't blame it on the fever because that was gone. But something—he doubted it was inherent business sense, since this had nothing to do with business—told him she was sincere. That his comfort was of concern to her and that it went beyond the fact that he was a potential client.

Or maybe he was just hallucinating. He tested the waters. "I believe you mean that."

T.J. cocked her head, as if that could somehow give her a better view of the inner workings of his mind. She would have been naive to believe that the toy business wasn't as cutthroat as any other competitive business, but if she'd had her druthers, she would have wanted to believe that it wasn't. Toys were the realm of children and nothing as jaded as cynicism should ever touch it.

What sort of people was he used to dealing with? "Why wouldn't I?"

He shrugged. The ridiculous blue nightshirt swished against his shoulder blades. "Because I'm a stranger."

She leaned the tray against the bureau and smiled. "Not really. Your people have talked to my people." Tongue in cheek, she teased, "In the nineties, that makes us practically family."

"Maybe." He didn't want her to leave. Not just yet. Christopher searched for something to say, for a way to make her remain just a moment longer. "You're nothing like what I expected."

"Oh?" She took a breath, knowing she should stop right here, right now. There was no point in having him elaborate. It would be just asking for trouble. But she'd come this far, and curiosity was pushing the buttons. "And what was it that you expected?"

He thought of the *People* magazine article his assistant had handed him just before he'd boarded his plane. Meant to supplement the report he already had on her, the article had been on Theresa Cochran and it was entitled "Beauty with Brains." He was in complete agreement with the assessment, but it didn't go far enough. Nowhere in the article did it mention the traits he'd been fleetingly privy to.

Without thinking, Christopher reached for her hand. Wrapping his fingers around it, he continued. "Someone less nurturing for one. Someone who didn't know her way around a kitchen." He thought of the scene in the family room. "Or a child."

Did he realize that he was rubbing his thumb along the pulse in her wrist, or was he doing that unconsciously? Whichever it was, she wished he'd stop. She didn't like the effect it was having on her knees.

"Always Be Prepared, that's my motto." Tactfully she disentangled herself.

Another piece of the puzzle presented itself to him. He tried to fit it in. Ordinarily he liked to know things about the people who worked for him only because then there was no room for surprises. He didn't like surprises. Until now.

"You were a Boy Scout?"

"No, a Girl Scout." A dimple flickered in the corner of her mouth. "Hey, we have Girl Scouts, even in Beverly Hills." She *had* been a Girl Scout. Theresa, on the other hand, had viewed the idea of camping and selling cookies as beneath her.

It occurred to him that he still didn't know where he had been brought. "Is that where I am? Beverly Hills?"

She didn't know just how much he knew about Theresa. Her estate was in the most expensive section of Beverly Hills. Finances as well as preference had dictated that T.J. choose a far more down to earth area to settle in.

"That's where the office is, and we're close to the office."

Was it him, or was she being deliberately vague in her answer? He decided that perhaps, in this case, he was being a bit too suspicious. He was accustomed to having to read between the lines. Rarely were things as aboveboard as they were here.

Picking up the tray again, T.J. began to leave. "So, can I get you anything else?"

The answer, "*You*" whispered along his mind like a soft spring breeze, surprising him.

For a moment, he thought he'd said it aloud, but her expression hadn't changed, so it must have been just his imagination. Something he was going to have to rein in. He hadn't come here to play pattycake with a stunning woman. He'd come here to give or withhold his final seal of approval to a new advertising firm.

But Christopher had to admit, if only to himself, that sick or not, the word *merger* was taking on a whole different meaning.

He was getting better fast.

There wasn't even a television set in the room. And he was restless. More so now that she was in the room, bringing the scent of spring in with her.

"I'm getting stir-crazy," he admitted. He was used to doing things, not lying flat on his back.

She smiled. "You're getting better." It took her only a moment to make up her mind. Any longer and she might have thought better of the idea. "How about if I let you graduate to the sofa?"

"Excuse me?"

Her tongue was getting ahead of her. He really was rattling her. "You can come into the family room and watch cartoons with Megan and me." She saw that the suggestion wasn't bowling him over, but if she was going to be around him, it was safer if she had something to divert her attention away from his eyes. Megan was the likeliest choice. "I have over twenty-four hours' worth of tapes for you to choose from if the programs that are on don't please you."

What the hell? He'd never watched Saturday-morning cartoons, even as a child. His nannies hadn't approved of "mindless animation." It might be interesting at that. At least he could say he'd actually done it once.

But something wasn't quite right with the picture. "That's an awful lot of cartoon tapes to keep for someone who doesn't live with you."

The dossier he'd received on her hadn't hinted that the woman who periodically turned up at parties on both sides of the Atlantic was someone who would watch cartoons or stock them for a niece. But then, it hadn't led him to believe that she was capable of rolling around on the floor with a two-year-old, either. And he had seen that with his own eyes.

The lady was full of surprises. Pleasant ones.

She was going to have to remain on her toes. It

made her feel weary. This, at least, was easy enough to explain away.

"Megan's here a lot. I send T.J. off regularly on business trips. She's very good at what she does." T.J. bit her lip, then decided that there was no harm in building herself up. What she said was, after all, all true. "She put together the campaign for MacAffee Toys."

He'd been told that, too. "I'm impressed." He knew he wouldn't have admitted that so readily if he wasn't in the process of recovering. Praise from him was hard-won and he doled out it slowly. Otherwise, whoever he was dealing with could capitalize on that and hold him at a disadvantage.

But somehow, slowly didn't seem to fit the situation here. "I'd like to meet her sometime."

Meet, as in return. The sinking feeling in the pit of her stomach was becoming a familiar sensation. "Oh, I thought this was just a one-time visit. You know, to look over the troops to see if they're battle fit."

He thought he detected nervousness in her voice and thought it rather odd. "That's the way I usually operate, but it's not something written in stone."

"I see." He wasn't supposed to return. It was what she and Theresa were counting on. So why did the thought of his returning bring such a rosy warmth with it? She had no time to analyze it or to upbraid herself for having ambivalent feelings. "Well, as I told you, T.J. is away this weekend. But I'm sure she'd be flattered by your assessment of her work if she were here."

Time to retreat before she tripped herself up. T.J. nodded at the tray in her hands. "Why don't I clear this away and see about getting things set up in the family room?''

There had already been a lot of time lost. Given a choice, he didn't want to waste any more watching cartoons. ''We really should—''

She knew where he was going with this. She also knew that she had promised Megan she'd watch TV with her. T.J. loathed to break a promise. ''I promise to have your briefcase in full view the entire time.'' She saw that Christopher's brows drew together. *Misstep.* Maybe he couldn't be teased about work. She reconnoitered. ''No one's going to take any points off if you kick back, you know.''

And with that, she left the room.

Well, so much for choice, Christopher thought. He didn't realize he was smiling until he saw his reflection in the wardrobe mirror.

WALKING INTO THE KITCHEN, T.J. sighed as she deposited the tray on the table. Mechanically she rinsed off the soup bowl before placing it into the dishwasher. That made it a full load, she noted.

Cecilia stood silently watching her and wasn't quite sure how to read what she saw. ''Well, you certainly don't look like a woman who's got a hell of a handsome-looking man in her bed.''

T.J. could feel a headache building just behind her eyes. ''That's just the problem.''

Cecilia laughed and shook her head. ''Never heard it called that before.'' She jerked her thumb in the general direction of T.J.'s room. ''That's the kind of 'problem' most women pray for. Have you taken a good look at that man?'' She covered her chest with her hand. "Makes my heart flutter just to think about him."

Notwithstanding the fact that Cecilia's view of male-female relations could stand a bit of updating, T.J. laughed. She shut the dishwasher door firmly and set the dials. The sound of rushing water followed. "He's too short for you."

At six-four, Cecilia had gotten used to the fact that most men were. "Good things come in small packages."

T.J. wondered how their houseguest would have reacted to being called small. And how he would react if he ever discovered that he was being duped.

"Not this time."

T.J.'s voice was definitely too pensive. Placing her hands on the younger woman's arms, Cecilia turned her around until they faced one another. "All right, give. What's wrong?"

Where did she begin? "He thinks I'm Theresa."

Cecilia's eyes narrowed. "I thought the whole idea was that he was *supposed* to think you're Theresa." And then it hit her. Clear as a tide pool in Miami. "Hey, wait a minute, you don't *want* him to think you're Theresa, do you?"

T.J. shrugged her hands away. Cecilia had a way of seeing too much. "I don't like lying."

There was more to it than that and they both knew it. Or at least one of them did, Cecilia thought. "It's all a matter of interpretation. Sometimes a little lie moves things along."

"Little?" T.J. echoed, then laughed shortly. "The man thinks I'm the president of C & C Advertising."

Cecilia didn't see what the big deal was. "And if

your father hadn't dropped out of the business world and disappeared into the African jungle, you might have been."

"South American jungle," T.J. corrected. An uncustomary impatience reared its head. "And I like my position at the firm just fine." She had no desire to be at the helm of the company. P.R. was Theresa's specialty, not hers. "That's not the problem."

Cecilia was grinning at her like someone who had the answer to the question in the bonus round.

"What?"

"You like him, don't you?" There was a God, Cecilia thought with relief. At one point, she'd despaired that T.J. would waste her life in what amounted to seclusion. The way she had. Surrounded by people, but alone.

T.J. wanted to deny it. Heatedly. But the truth was, she just didn't know. "Whether I do or not doesn't matter—" She made a futile attempt to discredit Cecilia's assumption. "And he hasn't been here long enough for me to form any opinions about him. I just feel like I'm trying to walk across quicksand."

Cecilia wrapped one long, comforting arm around T.J.'s shoulders. "Everyone knows you don't walk across quicksand, you sprint if you can't get around it any other way." She dropped her hand to her side. "Is he going to be eating dinner at the table with us?"

Where the man ate dinner didn't affect the quantity prepared. "If he feels up to it." She looked at Cecilia suspiciously. "Why?"

"No reason."

The expression on Cecilia's face was entirely too innocent and made T.J. feel uneasy. She prayed the woman wouldn't attempt to try her hand at matchmaking. The sooner Christopher MacAffee was on a plane back to San Jose, the better she'd feel.

"If you want to look at him, he's going to be sitting in the family room as soon as I find a tape to put into the machine." T.J. turned to leave.

Cecilia raised her voice, calling after her. "I could run to the video store and rent *Wild, Passionate Nights* for you."

T.J. hoped her houseguest hadn't heard that. "We'll probably be watching *Mr. Duck Goes to the City,* thank you." It was Megan's favorite.

Cecilia's mouth dropped open as she stared at T.J. incredulously. "A cartoon? You're going to have a gorgeous, unattached man sitting beside you on the sofa and you're going to be watching cartoons?"

She wasn't going to be drawn into a debate about this. "Yup."

Cecilia could only shake her head. "You don't believe in opening doors when opportunity pounds on them, do you?"

It was time to place kidding aside. "This is not an opportunity, Cecilia. I just want to get through this charade intact. The sooner he gets well and goes back to San Jose, the sooner I'll breathe easy."

The problem with experience, Cecilia thought with regret, was that you couldn't pass it on. No one wanted it secondhand. "I hear you, but I just can't believe you."

"You don't have to believe me, as long as I do."

The thing of it was, T.J. thought as she began to rummage through the drawers of the video cabinet in the family room, that she was beginning not to believe herself, either. Not completely, at any rate.

Since her divorce, she'd gone out a number of times socially, always with friends. Always with the thought of enjoying the evening and the company, but only in the spirit of friendship. She wasn't out for romance. Not anymore. She was much too busy these days and there were more important things in her life than the search for romance. Megan headed that list.

But there was something about Christopher MacAffee that cut through all the stories, all the excuses she had sold herself on. An excitement that bubbled up within her just at the very sight of him.

Damn, but she sounded like some teenager with a budding crush.

She was going to have to find a way to put a lid on that, she lectured herself sternly. Even if she were inclined to let things happen between them—which she wasn't—he thought she was Theresa. There was no future in getting close to a man who thought she was her cousin. You couldn't build a relationship on a lie. And she certainly couldn't tell him who she was now. If he found out the truth, he'd take his business and his indignant, bruised ego elsewhere. Nobody liked being fooled, least of all a man in a position of power.

Business was the bottom line here. She had to remember that.

T.J. sighed as she selected two tapes and pulled them out of the drawer. Talk about painting yourself into a corner.

"So what are we watching?"

She jumped, startled at the sound of his voice. The

tapes went clattering to the floor. Chagrined, she picked them up quickly.

She looked like a tax dodger who had just been summoned by the IRS. Christopher crossed to her, puzzled. "Hey, I didn't mean to sneak up on you. I thought I was supposed to be here."

She had to get hold of her nerves. Taking the first step, she smiled up at him. The family room was bathed in sunlight. It gave his complexion a healthy glow. Now that she thought about it, he did look a lot better. The man would definitely be on his way by tomorrow morning.

Why didn't that make her happy? Relieved, yes, but not happy. What was the matter with her, anyway?

"You are and you didn't," she assured him, though she doubted he bought the latter. "I was just preoccupied." The blue shirt he was wearing looked much better on him than Cecilia's nightshirt had. "I see you found your shirt."

He held out an arm, looking at the sleeve. "It's a better fit." Christopher lowered his voice, glancing toward the door to see if they were alone. "Just how tall is your housekeeper?"

"Six-four."

He readily believed it. "Sounds more like a bodyguard."

"She's my housekeeper," T.J. assured him. "Actually, Cecilia's more of a friend than anything else."

Tucking the tapes under her arm, she cleared off the oversize coffee table. She and Megan spent hours playing Candyland and putting simple puzzles together on it. Right now, the table was covered with papers, half-finished coloring books and scattered, chunky crayons.

Sitting down on the edge of the sofa, Christopher automatically began replacing the crayons into the empty crayon box he found under the table. "Where did you find her?"

"Christmas card," she answered absently. Glancing up, she saw that Christopher didn't understand. "We exchange them each year." T.J. backtracked further. "She was my gym teacher in high school. She went on to coach a girls' basketball team at UCI from there."

"Now that I believe." He tucked the lid flap into the crayon box. "How did she make the transition from coach to housekeeper?" It wasn't the kind of thing that readily came to mind.

Pleasure filled her voice as she spoke of the older woman. She had always gotten on well with Cecilia, even when their relationship had been teacher and student. "One Christmas, she wrote to fill me in. She'd given up coaching, didn't really have a place to call home." Cecilia didn't believe in owning things or letting things own her. She'd lived in a small trailer park until a developer bought the land out from under her. "I invited her to come stay with me. Then—"

T.J. almost slipped and said that it was just after she'd given birth to Megan. In her typical no-nonsense fashion, Cecilia had taken over running the household and helping her with Megan. Making life manageable. So much so that T.J. knew she'd be lost without the woman and her friendship.

"The rest is history." She held up the two tapes for his inspection. "*Mr. Duck Goes to the City.*" She turned one, then the other. "Or *Crickets in My Bed.* Take your pick."

Christopher looked at her to see if she was serious. She was. She was really going to show him cartoons. Someone else might have tried to impress him with a vast collection of the latest videotapes, or rushed to cull his favor by renting something a little more provocative. He rather liked the fact that she was being herself. And that "self" was someone who was apparently guileless and sure enough of herself to *be* herself.

"Which one does Megan like?"

He won points by bringing Megan into the decision. "*Mr. Duck.*" T.J. looked at the lime green cover on the tape. "She's seen it umpteen times."

He had trouble watching anything all the way through once, much less more. "And she doesn't get tired of it?"

T.J. thought he was kidding, then realized that he was serious. "You know, for someone in the toy business, you don't know very much about children. I think psychiatrists call it reinforcement. Familiar things give children a sense of security. All I know is that Megan likes to see things over and over again until she knows exactly what's coming."

She'd obviously taken the time to understand the little girl. As he saw it, that took an inordinate amount of patience as well as love. Something else that hadn't been in the report. "Megan's very fortunate to have you for an aunt."

She wished he'd stop complimenting her. She felt like such a fraud. T.J. lifted a careless shoulder. "Yeah, well, Megan is a pretty terrific little girl. I hope to have one like her someday,'' she added for good measure.

The party girl making domestic noises. He found that rather appealing. It made him stop and think about his own situation. Chronologically, he was more than ready to settle down. So far, though, he hadn't found the right woman....

Christopher realized he was staring at her and looked away.

Megan came tumbling into the room, chasing a mechanical poodle and laughing. He immediately became aware that the woman beside him lit up like a Christmas tree.

''Speak of the devil.'' T.J. held up the tape. ''Look what I have for you, Meggie.''

''Missy Duck!'' Megan crowed. She wrapped her hands around the videotape.

''Why don't you put it into the machine and we'll all watch it?'' T.J. suggested.

Megan whirled around on one sneakered heel and made a beeline for the machine nestled beneath a wide-screen television set.

Christopher had visions of the little girl jamming the tape into the VCR. ''Do you think you should let her handle that?''

T.J. grinned, watching Megan. Shaking the tape out of its cover, her daughter popped it into the slot. ''She knows how to operate the VCR. At least how to hit the play button.''

He leaned back on the sofa, making room for her. Jasmine again, he thought as she sat down beside him. Christopher filled his lungs with the sweet scent.

''We have something in common, then. You would

have had me worried if you'd said she knows how to get rid of the flashing twelve. That would have put her one up on me."

T.J. laughed. It was the same sparkling sound he'd heard earlier, when he had gone searching for the source. And it had the same effect on him now as it had then. More so. It reeled him in, a fish caught on a silver hook. Something within his gut tightened even as a warmth flowered all through him.

T.J. turned to look at him. The laughter died on her lips as her eyes met his. The cartoon theme song droning on in the background faded. There was nothing but silence in the room. Silence, except for the frantic beating of her heart, which had somehow managed to slip all the way up to her ears.

There was nothing else to do except give in to this incredible pull. If he explored it, maybe it would go away.

"I don't think I'm infectious anymore," Christopher said softly, his fingers slipping around her cheek, cupping her neck.

Her eyes couldn't leave his. "Oh, I wouldn't say that," she whispered through lips that were barely moving.

5

HE COULD SAY that he didn't know what came over him. That he was still a little disoriented by the virus. Any one of a number of excuses would have sufficed. But they would have all been lies.

Christopher knew exactly what came over him. She had. Theresa, with her laughter and her wit, with her warmth and her caring ways. It exuded from her without her having to say a word.

There was no recourse for him but to kiss her. It seemed his destiny, a destiny he readily embraced without wondering what the hell was going on in his mind. All he knew was that somewhere it was written that at this time, this place, Christopher MacAffee, scion of MacAffee Toys, was to kiss Theresa Cochran, president of C & C Advertising.

He would have bet his soul on it.

As soon as his lips touched hers, there was an inexplicable rush whirling through him, around him. Christopher felt he was being drawn into a vortex and there wasn't a single thing he could do about it.

And he wasn't all that sure that he wanted to.

The organizer within him, the man who was determined to make logical sense of everything, struggled to make sense out of this. Logic seemed to be out of order here. At the very least, it was taking a holiday.

This was just a kiss. Nothing more. He had to remember that. So what if he heard a rushing noise in his head and his body had suddenly ignited with a bittersweet agony he was in no position to do anything about? It was just a kiss. And if he felt unsteady, that was because of the virus, or the bug, or whatever the hell he'd come down with. It wasn't because of the kiss.

It couldn't be.

But it was.

Swallowing a groan, he deepened the kiss, determined not to be the only one bowled over here. His mouth played along hers, a concert pianist suddenly inspired to write a concerto.

T.J. didn't remember grabbing on to Christopher's arms to hang on, but she must have. Because she was. Hanging on for dear life. As if she were afraid that if she let go, she would be sucked under. Or blown away.

She was anyway.

Her fingers curled around the material of his sleeves, clutching.

This couldn't be happening. The thought desperately telegraphed itself through what was left of her mind. She refused to feel like this, as if she were hurtling down a steep mountainside atop those silly fiberglass sticks her cousin loved strapping onto her feet. But she was, hurtling fast and hard. Her breath was completely snatched away and her lungs were bursting for air.

This had to be what navigating without ski poles was like. She didn't like it.

It was far too exhilarating to be safe.

Christopher wanted to gather her into his arms, to feel her, to explore her until he knew his way around every inch of her body like a blind man touching a familiar, treasured object. He tried to remember when he'd last felt like this, and couldn't.

Because he hadn't. He'd never felt like this before. It would have scared him if he'd thought about it, but thinking had been the first thing to go.

"Mama kiss."

The childish voice, filled with glee, penetrated their consciousness simultaneously. The unexpected spontaneous combustion had made them both forget that they weren't alone.

They remembered now.

Reluctantly, Christopher drew his lips away from hers. He blinked as he held T.J. at arm's length, then looked at the small figure that was standing beside them, openly staring.

"Did she just call you Mama?" he asked, bewildered.

Oh, boy. Be cool, T.J., be cool. Think, for heaven's sake.

No easy feat when her brain felt like a scrambled egg on a hot skillet. She mustered a smile, then ran her hand along the little girl's arm affectionately.

"Maybe." T.J. looked at Christopher. "T.J. and I look a lot alike." Her explanation met with a cocked brow. "More than likely, though," she went on as her brain began to defog, "Megan was just saying that she's seen her mother kiss like this." Thank goodness Megan didn't speak in complete sentences yet.

"Not," Christopher assured her, "like this." She

had a one-two punch that had sent him reeling—and wanting more. It was a good thing that the child had interrupted when she had. He needed a breather to figure out just what had happened here. And what he wanted to happen in the future. "I'm beginning to understand why you have men lined up six deep on both sides of the continent."

"Yeah, well..." It took effort to sound nonchalant, but somehow, T.J. managed. "I think they're attracted to the business as much as to me."

She'd nearly said Theresa instead of "me." It was her personal theory that at least some of the men who flocked around Theresa were only after what being connected to the Cochran name could do for them. But it was all right because Theresa knew exactly who was after what. And in as much as she was after fun and nothing more, it all worked out for her.

T.J. knew she could never lead the kind of life Theresa did. Theresa was all bright reds and splashy colors. T.J. was subtle, muted blues. She was a nester and had been right from the beginning. She'd never cared for parties that lasted into dawn, or for being seen on the right arm. She liked quiet, intimate dinners and the love of one man, not the admiration of a squadron.

Which was why her breakup had hurt so badly. When she had exchanged vows with Peter, she had meant forever. Peter, on the other hand, had obviously meant to the end of the month. That was how long it had taken him before he'd found someone else to dally with. Someone to break his vows with.

"Really?" Christopher couldn't see how any man in his right mind would have wanted her for any other reason than because she was a beautiful, sensuous woman who was capable of heating a man's blood at ten paces. "Why do you put up with it?"

She gave him Theresa's stock answer. "Because I'm not taken in by it. I'm just out to have fun." T.J. needed backup. She patted the place beside her on the sofa. "Come here, Cupcake." T.J. looked at Megan. "Come sit up here."

Christopher noted that she placed the little girl between them.

Just as well, he thought. He didn't believe in mixing business with pleasure. Which was why, he supposed, there was very little pleasure in his life lately. The last couple of years it had seemed consumed by business.

Maybe, he mused, looking at Theresa, it was time that stopped.

Megan wiggled into a comfortable position on the sofa, then flashed a killer smile at him that was very reminiscent of her aunt's. Like a queen, she pointed her finger at the screen and ordered him to watch by loudly announcing, "Missy Duck."

"Mr. Duck," he corrected automatically.

Megan nodded, her brown curls bouncing around her head like coiled springs being shaken out of a bag. "Missy Duck."

Laughing to himself, Christopher gave up the language lesson and settled back to watch.

Much to his amazement, he discovered that he liked cartoons. At least the one Theresa had selected for them to watch.

Bright blue credits soon rolled up against a blazing white background, accompanied by the song Mr.

Duck always sang to himself when times got rough for him. Was the cartoon over already?

Christopher glanced at his watch in disbelief. He'd been sitting here for almost ninety minutes. Time seemed to have just flown by.

Curious, T.J. had looked over Megan's head several times to see if Christopher was actually watching. Each time she was surprised and pleased to see that he was. She didn't exactly know why she got a kick out of that, but she did.

"So, what did you think?" Pointing the remote at the VCR, she pushed the stop button. The credits abruptly disappeared, to be replaced with a black-and-white rerun of a popular late-sixties sitcom. It was about cousins who looked enough alike to be twins. T.J. quickly hit the power button and the set faded into darkness.

Christopher looked at Megan. She had sat stock-still for the entire movie, mesmerized as if she had never seen it before. But now she was all unharnessed energy. She dove toward the VCR to reclaim the tape. Obviously something her aunt had taught her, he thought.

He smiled at the question. "Kind of like a morality play with feathers."

The description tickled her. "It's never too early to instill basic decent principles in kids."

"I certainly can't argue with that."

Out of the corner of her eye, she saw Megan slip the tape back into its box. Leaving it on the floor, the little girl began to play with the castle she'd abandoned earlier. T.J. shifted in her seat, facing Christopher. She tucked one leg under her. It was time to mix in a little business.

"I like the fact that MacAffee Toys doesn't go in for flooding the market with action figures associated with blood-and-guts video games." It was gratifying, in this time when the dollar was the bottom line, to find a company with such integrity.

It had never occurred to Christopher to conduct business any other way. He was a great believer in tradition.

Christopher's mouth curved when he thought of the alternative. "I'd have several generations of ancestors spinning around in their graves if I did that."

She leaned her elbow against the sofa and propped her hand against her head, studying him. There was more to it than that.

"You don't strike me as a man who would be all that worried about nocturnal visitations from reprimanding ghosts." He was the type to do what he wanted. That he wanted to maintain a tradition brought up his personal stock with her.

The trouble was, she caught herself thinking, his stock with her was already too high.

He told her what she already instinctively knew. "No, but I believe in the credo myself."

"Good toys for good children." The motto was written across the top of each box that housed a MacAffee Toy. Her smile was soft, gentle. "A bit outdated sounding for the fast-track children of the nineties, but the sentiment is timeless."

It felt right, sitting here, talking to her like this. Even though the topic was business, it felt more intimate than that. He raised a speculative brow. "Are you trying to butter me up?"

Was that what he thought? She looked up into his eyes and decided that he was just teasing her. "No, I'm speaking the truth."

She had eyes, he thought, that a man could go wading in. Deep, fathomless, gorgeous eyes. It took him a moment to realize that she had said something, and another moment to replay it in his mind so he could respond.

"I know. That's why I've decided to go with you. Your company," he amended, lest either of them misunderstand. He was talking business. But there was a part of him that *really* wanted to go with her. Somewhere dark and romantic. And isolated.

There was something in his eyes that she found unsettling. Something that was reaching out to her on a far different level than the verbal one they were on.

She was having trouble keeping her mind on the conversation. T.J. reminded herself that business was the only thing that mattered here and the only reason she was having a conversation with Christopher in the first place.

"I'm flattered. Without even reviewing the rest of the campaign?"

He had already looked over all the preliminary drawings and proposals before flying down to meet with her. And he had no corrections to offer. It was as if they were of one mind about the direction he wanted the ad campaigns to go. But he did want to hear what Theresa had to add, if anything.

"Call it icing on the cake." If he didn't get off this sofa, he was going to reach out and kiss her again.

Christopher got up. "I'd really like to get down to work right now."

She nodded, relieved that he didn't try to kiss her again. And disappointed.

"Your call." She bit her lip. "Are you sure you're feeling up to it?"

The grin he gave in response to her question had color rushing to her cheeks. Yes, he'd proven that he was certainly over whatever had laid him low. No sick man could have kissed like that.

Tactfully, he made no reference to their kiss. "After watching *Mr. Duck Goes to the City,* I think I'm ready for anything."

"Well, then," she said breezily, rising to her feet, "let's get to it, shall we?" She gestured him out of the room. Her den, where she did most of her work, was located at the rear of the house. "Cecilia," T.J. called, glancing over her shoulder to see if Megan was still occupied. She was, but that could change at any moment.

Within a minute, the housekeeper appeared, filling the hall with her presence.

She'd been pretty once, Christopher thought, studying Cecilia's profile as she walked by him. He'd go so far as to venture that she'd been a knockout. She was still a striking woman.

He thought of Lester, his father's chauffeur. Lester hadn't been the same since his wife, Edith, had died. Edith had been a tall woman, though not as tall as Cecilia. He saw resemblance between the two women and wondered if Lester would be interested in meeting Cecilia.

The thought stunned him. What the hell was coming over him? He'd never thought of matching people up before. It had to be this house. There was a warmth here that permeated everything. And Theresa, he realized, was its source.

Cecilia let her eyes wash over Christopher approvingly before she looked at T.J. "You called?"

T.J. nodded. "Would you mind watching Megan for a while, please? Mr. MacAffee and I have a little business to go over."

Cecilia lowered her voice as she walked into the room. "Yes, I know. I saw a glimpse of negotiations when I passed by earlier."

T.J. flushed. She let the comment go. Saying anything in her defense would only lead to further embarrassment. Her eyes darted toward Christopher's face. Had he heard? He had and was apparently amused.

That made one of them.

"This way," she muttered, leading the way to the den.

IT WAS A SMALL ROOM that caught a corner of the sun when it set in the evening. Because the afternoon was dreary, T.J. had turned on the lights. There were several of Megan's drawings, Christopher noted, tacked strategically onto the bulletin board behind her desk. There was a bookcase against one wall, but the room was dominated by a desk. There wasn't much room for anything else.

She had a computer. State-of-the-art, from the looks of it. But it was dormant. She seemed to prefer drawing by hand. All the sketches she had spread across her desk for his perusal were hand drawn. He liked that. It seemed more personal that way and that was what his company had always striven for. The personal touch. It was how they had managed to survive in a world where everyone else was in the fast lane, scrambling toward the next goal. The perpetual race had created a void, a backlash. His company capitalized on the need it generated. Nostalgia had people wanting to return to the toys of their youth, of their parents' youth. And his company was there to fulfill that desire.

She'd insisted that he sit at her desk, utilizing the only chair in the room while she moved about before him, making what amounted to an impromptu presentation. And doing it brilliantly.

He was fascinated. She didn't just use her mouth when she spoke, but her entire body. Hand gestures, facial expressions, eyes that glinted and lit. She was a symphony of motion. And he found himself wanting to buy a season's ticket to the concert.

Christopher congratulated himself on finding the right person to do justice to his company. And maybe, he mused, he'd found a little more than that.

It bore further exploring.

Finished, T.J. waited and then frowned to herself. Christopher had just sat there, listening to her for over twenty minutes. She knew he was awake because his eyes were opened. But he hadn't commented or given her any input whatsoever on the work she'd placed before him. Had she managed to bore him into a coma?

Bridling her frustration, she still allowed a sigh to escape. "You're not saying anything."

She'd completely mesmerized him. "That's because you're still talking."

T.J. gathered her drawings together. They represented a great deal of late-night work, and she was proud of them. She wanted him to be proud of them, too. Very much so. Maybe she was asking too much.

"I'm done," she said quietly.

He nodded, pleased at what he'd been shown. "Then I'm impressed."

It was just too simple. She'd heard that he was a hard man to win over. Maybe she'd missed something. Maybe he was just toying with her for some perverse reason. It wouldn't be the first time. "And you're still going to sign with us?"

He wouldn't have pegged her as being insecure. Not from what he'd heard. Hurricane Theresa, they called her. Hurricanes weren't insecure. So far, not much of the report he'd received on her rang true. Except that she had great insight into what his company needed.

"More than ever."

She blew out a breath. She had done it. She'd clinched the deal. Theresa was going to be very happy about this. Her cousin had actively been after MacAffee Toys ever since Christopher's company had terminated its association with Random Ads.

"That's a relief."

Her reaction puzzled him a little. "I didn't think you'd care that much." He rose to stand beside her. She was a petite woman, he thought, with delicate bone structure that begged for a man's hand to caress worshipfully. "Acquiring new clients must be routine by now."

"It's never routine," she answered, quickly covering her slip. Theresa never seemed eager about anything, except maybe the hunk of the month, and then only at the beginning of the month.

Christopher liked her response. He found it refreshing. "Maybe that's why MacAffee Toys is going with you. You seem like you care." He looked down into her face and wondered fleetingly what it would be like if she cared for him. "You're awfully good at this. Blending work and play."

It was all she could do not to take a step back. He was standing way too close to her for comfort. She couldn't help wondering if he was referring to the kiss in the family room. For her part, she couldn't think of anything else for long and was surprised that she had even managed to make the presentation at all. Her pulse still felt like scrambled radio waves of a long-lost transmission endlessly traveling through space.

"And even finding time for your niece," he added when she didn't say anything.

He *was* talking about the kiss, she thought, suddenly nervous. What else could he be referring to? That was what "play" meant to him. Small wonder. Theresa had a reputation for going from man to man.

For a loquacious woman, she was being unusually quiet. Unable to help himself, he wove his fingers through her hair, combing it away from her face. "I don't think I've ever met anyone quite like you before."

Guilt took a giant step forward. "Maybe you're not meeting anyone like me now," she murmured under her breath.

What she said didn't make any sense. He had to have misheard her. "What?"

Damn it, she was going to have to stop feeling guilty about this. There was nothing to feel guilty about. This was business, pure and simple. It wasn't as if she was trying to reclaim the throne of Russia by posing as the long-lost Anastasia. She was just filling in for her cousin.

"Nothing." T.J. took a deep breath that sounded uncomfortably shaky to her ear. And the words were hard to push out. He had to stop touching her like that. "T.J. will be very pleased that you liked her work."

"These are T.J.'s?" He'd gotten the impression that she had personally drawn each one.

"Yes. I just make the presentations."

"And very convincingly. One would have thought they were yours."

His eyes were definitely too familiar, she thought. What made it worse was that she was enjoying it. And what made it worse than that was that he thought he was looking at Theresa.

She wished she'd never let herself be talked into this. With effort, she managed to move aside, stepping away from him. The back of her legs bumped against the desk.

"I'll let her know you liked them when she gets back." Her mouth felt dry. Turning, she began straightening papers that had already been straightened.

She almost sounded skittish. It had to be his imagination. Someone with her reputation was as far from skittish as he was from being a biker. Pleased with the way things had turned out, he felt like celebrating. With her.

"I'd like to take you out to dinner tonight."

An intimate table for two. Soft lights. Maybe music. She didn't think she could handle that. "That's not necessary."

He caught her arm as she moved past him. "No, please, I insist." She opened her mouth to protest again. Christopher deftly headed her off before she could. "To cement relations."

She wondered which he meant and hated herself for knowing which she wanted him to mean. Those relations had already gone further than she'd ever dreamed.

T.J. tried to get him to change his mind. "Are you sure you wouldn't just rather stay in? You know, gather your strength together to fly home tomorrow?" It annoyed her that in her heart, she wanted him to stay. But she did. "You were pretty sick yesterday."

If he didn't know better, he would have said she was trying to get rid of him. But he did know better. Call it gut instinct, but he had a feeling that the woman before him wasn't the type to lie or use people. She was just being concerned. He liked that. Probably more than he should.

"It really did turn out to be just a twenty-four-hour bug. I feel great now." More than that, he felt as if he'd never been sick at all. "And I won't take no for an answer."

She smiled up into his face while her stomach turned to Jell-O. "Well, then I guess I won't give it." *Although I know I really should.*

6

"THIS WASN'T REALLY necessary, you know."

T.J. raised her eyes to Christopher's across the table. Dinner had been far more pleasant than she had expected. Deciding to take out all the stops and play Theresa to the hilt, she discovered that she thoroughly enjoyed the role. Maybe more than she should.

She told herself that it was just for the night and since he already believed that she was her cousin, there was no harm being done. The wine she'd had with her meal helped mute her conscience.

Christopher couldn't remember when he'd enjoyed himself so much. And in such a simple place. "I think it was."

She leaned her head on her upturned palm. The wine had taken a path straight to her head, stripping inhibitions away as it went. "Oh, you did, did you?"

"Yes." He wanted to repay her for kindness that had gone over and above the call of duty. That, and spend some time with her. He glanced around the family restaurant. It was fairly full. They'd been lucky to get a booth off to the side. "What I didn't think was that you'd be caught dead in a steak house."

Theresa wouldn't have. She wouldn't have eaten a steak unless the menu proclaimed it to be filet mignon and thirty dollars a cut. But T.J.'s tastes ran in a less complex direction. Adroitly, she covered her slip by flirting. The more she did it, the more natural flirting seemed to her. And the more she enjoyed it.

"You seem to have a lot of preconceived notions about me."

"Some." Other notions, he thought, were brand-new. And growing in volume.

She toyed with the last of her baked potato. Strangely, her appetite had all but disappeared, but she felt full. Full and light at the same time. There was a rush that came over her when she looked at him that frightened her. The only way she could savor it was by taking refuge in her role.

"Homework?" she guessed, smiling.

What would he say if he knew that he wasn't sitting across from the subject of the report she knew was sitting somewhere in his office? For one wild moment, she was tempted to tell him, just to see his reaction. But then she would have to give up the charade, not to mention suffer the consequences for it. This was much better. Safer.

And more exciting.

He spread his hands expansively. Some women would have resented the intrusion. But Theresa Cochran was more sophisticated than that. She knew it went with the territory.

"All right, you caught me. I believe in thoroughly knowing who I'm dealing with." He studied her face and knew that he'd guessed correctly. She didn't mind. "Don't you?"

"Yes and no." Her mind elsewhere, she let her eyes glide over his lips and relived the moment he'd kissed her.

He hadn't kissed *her,* she reminded herself. Christopher had kissed Theresa. She knew it was the wine that was creating the small, sharp prick of jealousy she felt, but that didn't make it any less hurtful.

"I like surprises," she elaborated, her voice deep, husky.

There was an impish gleam in her eyes. He just bet she did, he thought. It seemed her style.

"I didn't. Until now." The corners of his mouth pulled into a grin. He found her incredibly easy to talk to. Something else he hadn't expected. "You've turned out to be quite a pleasant one."

Ambivalent feelings warred within her. Theresa would have coyly laughed here, absorbing the compliment as her due. T.J. couldn't quite bring it off. Guilt wouldn't allow it. Conscience made her want to warn him. "Maybe you're just jumping to conclusions."

Modest, too. Now there was a surprise. It just kept getting better and better. "I don't think so. I'm a fairly good judge of character."

Leaning over, Christopher topped off her wine, finishing the bottle. He debated asking for another, then decided against it. He wanted a clear head tonight. He had a feeling that it might be a long while before it was over.

A good judge of character? Not hardly, T.J. thought. She took a sip before answering. When she did, she gestured with her glass. "May I remind you that most of your judging time has been spent under covers, comatose."

"Some things you just have a gut feeling about." He placed a hand over hers on the table. There was an intimacy between them in this noisy, brightly lit steak house. He felt it far more strongly than on the occasions when he brought a companion to a posh, romantically dim restaurant. It was the woman and not the place. "Like the fact that this merger is going to be a good one. I think your firm can do a great deal for mine."

She raised her glass in a silent toast, reinforcing his words. "No doubt about that. We have a great many ideas to put into motion."

His eyes skimmed over her. She was wearing a simple black dress with the air of a princess swaddled in velvet. He had a feeling she could bring off wearing burlap. "Suddenly, so do I."

Oh, boy. T.J. took a long sip this time, fortifying herself. She could plainly read what was on his mind. Perhaps because it was on hers, too. And it shouldn't be.

Christopher drew back a little. This was far too public a place to indulge in displays of affection. He wasn't certain what had come over him. Being with Theresa appeared to loosen him up. It was something, he realized, that he could get used to.

"You don't know what a relief it is, meeting someone like you. I can relax, without worrying that perhaps it's MacAffee Toys you find attractive—"

Her eyes widened in surprise before she remembered she was supposed to be sultry. She slanted her gaze. "Instead of you?"

Had all the women in his life been blind up to now? He was gorgeous. If she had met him as herself instead of Theresa, he would have been the one to make her want to give romance another chance.

But she hadn't met him as herself. She'd met him as Theresa and she was stuck with that. There wasn't anything she could do to change that now.

Christopher lifted his shoulders, then let them drop carelessly. "Well, I wasn't going to put it exactly that way." He felt a little foolish. "I'm not always that good with words."

"You're doing just fine." Maybe too fine, she added silently. It was getting increasingly harder to remember just where the line was drawn between role-playing and reality. Her mind kept drifting, as did her feelings. Having him extol her "honesty" wasn't making things any easier on her.

He slowly twirled the wine stem. The overhead light reflected in the pink liquid, making it gleam. Christopher studied it before continuing. He wasn't accustomed to baring his feelings. But somehow he thought she'd understand.

"You'd be surprised at how many women have ulterior motives when it comes to relationships. Not that I've had the time for that many in the last few years."

There was more here than that. There had been a flicker of sadness in his eyes. Compassion made T.J. forget to feel uncomfortable. "But the one you did find time for ended badly?" Empathy filled her. She remembered the pain when she'd discovered the truth about Peter.

"You might say that." He finished his glass, then set it down beside hers. "I fell hard."

He was being unabashedly honest with her, more than he'd ever been with people he'd known most of his life. Funny how he felt closer to this woman he hadn't known forty-eight hours ago than he did to his friends. But there was so much understanding in her eyes, it drew him out.

And in.

"She, on the other hand, fell for my name and my bankbook. And the family connections." Christopher looked at her. "Do you ever run into that?" She'd mentioned something about it earlier, but he thought she was just making polite conversation. He couldn't imagine anyone using her.

T.J. thought of Theresa. Of the jet-setting life she managed to conduct along with a fair amount of business. And of the men who swarmed around her cousin. In comparison, there were times she felt like the family ugly duckling, even though they were essentially cut out of the same cloth. They looked alike, but it was Theresa's zest for life, her flair that made her beautiful. There were times, just a few, when she had envied Theresa her free and easy style, her way of drawing the fun out of life and discarding the rest.

With sobering determination, T.J. reminded herself that she had Megan and a career she loved. That was enough for her.

It *was,* she insisted silently, trying to negate the power of his gaze.

With the air of a conspirator, she leaned into Christopher, lowering her voice as she resumed her role. "Do I ever run into that? All the time."

"I guess that gives us something in common." He thought that over for a moment. "Actually, we have a great deal in common." He saw by the look in her eyes that she was unconvinced. "We both helm family businesses, both are only children and both have to glean the wheat from the chaff.''

And we're both unattached, he added silently.

''Except that you're all business and I'm not.'' *Oh, and just one more tiny little thing. I'm not who you think I am.*

He inclined his head. Maybe it was the place, or the humbling effect of waking up to find himself in a flowing nightshirt. More than likely, it was the company. The light in her eyes, the husky laugh. All of which made him want to turn over a new leaf. To finally enjoy the life he'd been so busy rushing through.

''Maybe I shouldn't be. All business, that is. I don't have to be,'' he corrected. ''Not with the right person.''

Completely sobered now, T.J. looked down at her plate, wishing there was a way to disappear. What was he going to say when he found out that he'd been pouring his heart out to a fraud? A phony? She felt for him. And for herself.

T.J. did the only thing she could—she diverted him with work. Desperate, she grabbed on to the first thought that surfaced. ''You know, speaking of the right person, I've been thinking. Valentine's Day is less than two weeks away—''

''I know.'' He cocked his head. What was she getting at?

She lowered her eyes. This wasn't going to come out at all if she was looking at him. He had a way of making her mouth grow dry. ''If we hurry, we can launch a TV campaign a couple of days before it hits—''

"A Valentine campaign for MacAffee Toys?" Humor twisted his mouth. "Toys aren't generally associated with Valentine's Day."

"No, but stuffed animals are." Mercifully, the idea began to take form in her head. As far as she knew, there were no commercials featuring stuffed animals for the day. That was strictly the domain of flowers and candy. "I was going through your catalog last night. You've got several items that would make wonderful gifts for men to give to the women in their lives."

Warming to her subject, her enthusiasm grew. "For instance, that white bear you have. The one that says, 'I wuv you' when you squeeze it." Pulling a pen out of her purse, she made a quick sketch on her napkin, turning it around for Christopher to look at. "It's perfect. We could say something like, 'Can't find the words to tell her? This Valentine's Day, send an emissary in your place.' And then we can feature the bear."

He laughed, amused, but he was taken with the idea. Her enthusiasm was infectious. Just like she was. "So that the lady in question can think she's getting a message from Elmer Fudd?"

She grinned. "Trust me, all women love stuffed animals."

Her eyes were shining. Did she like stuffed animals? It seemed almost incongruous. "I would have thought you preferred jewelry."

Theresa adored anything that sparkled and came in carats. T.J., on the other hand, had a weakness for plush.

"There's room for both. As an added touch, you

could have the bear holding a diamond ring box in its paws. They could be tied around it with a bright red ribbon.'' Hastily she added a few more lines to the drawing. It was of a woman hugging a man, a toy bear dangling from her fingers. ''So, what do you think?''

''I like it.'' It would open up a whole brand-new avenue for them. ''Get on it.''

''Consider it done.'' She beamed, pleased. And then remembered. Nothing had been formalized. They were getting ahead of themselves. ''We have contracts to sign first.''

Christopher waved the obstacle away. ''A formality I'll have taken care of before the end of the week. I've already had our lawyers draw up preliminary papers.''

She leaned back, looking at him. ''So you were pretty sure you were going with us?''

Experience had him answering cautiously. ''Not really. I wanted to check you out myself. I don't believe in dealing with companies whose CEOs don't care about the quality of the work, only the money it generates. You've completely won me over.'' He put his hand out to seal the bargain.

Something fluttered inside her as she slipped her hand into his. It was pleasure, mingled with satisfaction and a degree of anticipation, that overwhelmed her.

Christopher didn't break the connection immediately. Instead, he sat, holding her hand, savoring feelings that had nothing to do with the bargain their lawyers and accountants would ultimately solidify.

They had to do with a man sitting across from a beautiful woman.

He raised his glass. There was only a drop left in it, but he toasted the merger anyway. "Here's to a long association."

She touched her empty glass to his. She fervently hoped it wasn't prophetic that they were toasting with empty glasses.

"Amen to that." *And may you never find out that we pulled something over on you.*

He felt the flutter in her wrist as he released her hand. "You seem nervous. Do I make you nervous?" It didn't seem possible, and yet…

Maybe a pinch of honesty would placate him. "No, *I* make me nervous."

That was enigmatic. "Why?"

The words just seemed to fall from her lips of their own accord. T.J. hadn't meant to be this open, but once she began, there was no way of gracefully turning back.

"Because I'm having all these thoughts I shouldn't be having."

His eyes held hers. The amusement in them slowly faded into something far more intense. "About?"

She had come this far, she might as well admit the rest. Or as much as she could. She couched it in terms that Theresa might have used. "Mixing business with pleasure."

He watched in fascination as her long, sooty lashes swept along the swell of her cheeks. Christopher felt something tighten in his gut. "Funny. Me, too."

It would be so easy to let things just evolve....

Easy, but not right. T.J. drew herself up. ''But we can't.''

Reserve? Christopher hadn't expected that. ''Why not? Sometimes these things work out.''

She thought of the consequences that loomed ahead if they were to become involved. ''Not this time.''

She was far more reticent than he would have thought. Shy even. The lady was a box just filled with surprises—each more pleasing than the last, Christopher decided.

His eyes caressed her face. He liked the light that rose in her eyes, and the tiny, nervous flutter he detected in her throat. This wasn't an act she was putting on for his benefit. This was genuine. Christopher found himself charmed all over again.

''You'll never know until you try.''

Her mind scrambled for a way out. She thought of the conversation. ''I don't want you to think that I'm seducing you for your business.''

A couple passing their table just then looked from Christopher to T.J. and shook their heads disapprovingly as they moved on.

T.J. sank down in her seat, but laughter bubbled in her throat. ''They probably think I'm propositioning you.'' The thought of her propositioning anyone was completely ludicrous.

And yet, he was generating these unfamiliar feelings within her. Reckless, delicious feelings.

''Instead of the other way around.'' He didn't want her misunderstanding. This had nothing to do with business. ''And we've already sealed the deal, so anything that happens between us is after the fact.''

He looked at his empty plate and the empty glass

beside it. Suddenly Christopher knew exactly what he wanted for dessert. He was rarely so sure of anything outside of business. But he was sure of this.

It just felt right.

Nodding at her place setting, Christopher asked, "Ready to go?"

"Yes."

The answer, she knew, had come a little too quickly and perhaps breathlessly. But she wanted to be out of here, away from the setting of just the two of them and back home, where there was Megan and Cecilia and a shower that had cold water. She planned to stand under the shower head for a few hours.

Picking up her purse, she slid out of the booth. Christopher was beside her by the time she rose to her feet. He slipped his arm around her shoulders and guided her out. He'd already paid the bill before the food had ever arrived. There were some advantages to eating in a steak house, he mused, glad the mood could continue unbroken.

As they walked out the door, he thought he felt her shaking. It couldn't be because she was nervous. Theresa Cochran was too sophisticated for that. And yet, it wasn't cold out. On the contrary, the night was warm and sultry, adding to his mood.

Another explanation occurred to him as he directed her toward her car at the far end of the lot. "Theresa, are you feeling all right? You're not coming down with what I had, are you?"

It was her way out.

She wanted to jump at the excuse. But she was already hip deep in lies. She didn't want to add to the pile any more than she already had.

"No." Reaching the car, she turned toward him. When she raised her eyes to his, her expression was somber. "I don't think we should take this any further." She'd never hated saying anything more in her life. But it was for the best.

Had he misinterpreted the signs? No, he was better at reading people than that. Christopher searched her face for a clue. "Why?"

Theresa could have come up with something, created a dozen excuses. T.J. could only whisper the truth. "Because I want it too much."

Funny how six simple words could change his life. He'd never been a public creature, never one to display his feelings. But that didn't seem to matter right now. Unmindful of where they were, and of the fact that there were people coming and going in the lot, Christopher gathered her to him.

His arms felt as if they belonged around her. As if she belonged against him. His body needed the warmth that hers generated. Inhaling deeply, he drew the fragrance of her hair into his lungs.

"I understand."

She looked at him uncertainly. Anticipation trembled within her. What was she doing, jeopardizing everything because the touch of his hand made her heart flip-flop? After tonight, she was never going to see the man again. She didn't subscribe to the "Two ships in the night" theory.

And here she was, wanting him to touch her. To want her. To make love with her.

She had to be crazy.

"You do?" she asked.

He nodded. "You're afraid to surrender to your emotions. You always have to be in control."

Boy, was he wrong. She opened her mouth to protest, but he laid a finger against her lips.

"I know," he confided, "because I'm the same way. But it doesn't have to be about surrendering control. No one has to be in control. It can just be about two people enjoying each other."

He made it sound so simple. If only it were, she thought in despair. If only she had met him as herself, instead of as Theresa.

Guilt and desire warred with one another. Guilt won. But she had an uneasy feeling that it might not be a permanent victory.

Worse, that she didn't want it to be.

"Funny, that sounds like something I would say." Or that Theresa would say, she amended silently.

"See? We're of one mind. The more I talk to you, the more alike we turn out to be."

"Incredible, isn't it?" Her laugh sounded a bit hollow to her ear.

"*Incredible* is the word for it." And for her. His voice was soft, and the look in his eyes as he lowered his mouth to hers threatened to make her heart stop altogether.

Feelings took over. Without waiting for him to make contact, she rose on her toes and buried her hands in his hair. An eagerness she was unaccustomed to filled her as she pressed her lips to his.

And then she was completely swept away.

She never stood a chance. She didn't want one. She wanted, instead, to have this wonderful, wild, heady feeling to completely drain all thoughts, all feeling of guilt and deception away from her.

T.J. felt his hands along her back, pressing her to him, felt the leap of joy as he deepened the kiss until it anesthetized her. She felt limp even as her blood roared through her veins.

She was trembling again, he thought, mystified. Or was that him? He didn't feel his knees. A first. Christopher had never been shaken up by a woman before. It was an experience he would have found frightening if it wasn't so thoroughly enjoyable.

He tasted the wine on her lips. Wine and desire. It was a hell of a heady combination, but he thought he could handle it. And do it justice.

Her heart pounding madly, T.J. managed to place her hands on his arms and push herself back. An ache of regret accompanied her words. "I think we'd better be getting back, don't you?"

"I'm not sure I can. I didn't drop any bread crumbs to mark my way."

Oh, please let him be talking about where she lived and not about his emotions. Because she felt it, too. She tried to ignore the thrill that created.

T.J. opened the driver's side and got in. "That's all right. I'm the one driving and I remember the way back."

Flipping the lock open on his side from the control panel, she silently added, *Maybe.*

7

CHRISTOPHER HAD ALWAYS exercised extreme caution in his relationships. Suspicion of motives had been second nature for him. It was the way his father had raised him. He thought it was the way things would always be.

There were no suspicions now. It was as if something had fallen away from him. A protective glass shield. A force field around his heart. He had no desire to be guarded.

The woman beside him in the car completely captivated him. She was everything he had ever wanted in a woman: smart, funny, resourceful, nurturing. A sexy Mary Poppins with a dash of Andrew Carnegie's business acumen. Hell, what more could a man want?

To build on the foundation before him, Christopher thought. That was what a man could want. It was what he wanted.

He was never slow about making up his mind. And he'd made it up this evening.

All things considered, the steak house had been an improbable place to find himself falling in love.

Improbable, but not impossible. It had to be love, he reasoned, because he'd never felt anything like this before.

He wanted to take her dancing along the banks of

the River Thames. To Paris to sip wine in the shadow of the Eiffel Tower. To Tahiti to make love on the beach. He felt wild, reckless, none of which he could even vaguely remember feeling before. It had to be love. Or total insanity.

Maybe, he mused, watching her profile, it was a little bit of both.

They were almost home. If T.J. weren't driving, it would have been a struggle for her not to knot her fingers together in her lap. It wasn't something Theresa would do. Theresa would never have allowed an outward display of nerves to be witnessed. T.J. didn't think Theresa was even capable of being nervous. They were very different in that respect.

What did Theresa have to be nervous about, anyway? She led a charmed life. That was because her cousin knew that she would always be there to bail her out. T.J.'s jaw clenched as she turned onto her street.

Well, maybe she was sick of being the dependable one. Good old dependable T.J., always living in Theresa's shadow.

But tonight was different. Tonight she was Cinderella. Or Theresa, she amended. She glanced at Christopher and saw that he was looking at her. Warmth bathed her all over again. T.J.'s stomach quavered as she offered him a wide smile.

What the hell? If he thought she was Theresa, then she was going to *be* Theresa. All the way. And tomorrow, when he was on his plane, flying away from her and into forever, she would revert back to being dependable, safe, unexciting T.J.

But right now there was tonight.

She shifted in her seat, chafing, anxious. Anticipation marched through her like a well-drilled military band playing John Philip Sousa's *Stars and Stripes Forever.* The seat belt dug into her shoulder, a reminder that things were best played safe. Should she? Should she just continue being safe? Or should she, just once in her life, grab the brass ring and run with it? No one would know the difference.

They wouldn't, she thought, slanting another glance at Christopher, even know it was her.

Temptation whispered seductively in her ear. Would Christopher do the same if she let him? Would his warm breath skim along her skin when he spoke?

That was something, T.J. decided, she really wanted to find out. A smile curved her mouth as her blood began to hum with mounting excitement. Desire was winning the battle against common sense.

Guiding the car into the driveway, she pulled up the hand brake and turned toward him.

"You're awfully quiet." He'd hardly said anything on the way home. "Was it something I said?"

He'd been content just watching her. Just watching the shadows from the towering trees that lined the neighborhood streets play over her face as streetlights shone through them.

"Everything you said."

Uh-oh. One layer of her newly applied bravado began slipping away. But the look on his face told her that everything was still all right.

"Actually, I was just thinking how funny fate is."

Yes, it was a riot, all right. Otherwise, how would they have ever wound up here, in front of her door, contemplating a step she'd never taken so rapidly before? Covering the sudden burst of nerves dancing through her, T.J. opened her door and got out.

"Oh?" She tried to keep her voice nonchalant, light. Her stomach felt as if it were knotting up.

Getting out on his side, Christopher looked at her over the roof of the navy car. "I almost didn't come down here to meet you," he admitted.

She didn't understand. It was his practice to conduct these interviews. And his father had done it before him. "But you always—"

He nodded, casually slipping his arm through hers as they came up the walk. "Yes, that's just it. I 'always,' just like my father 'always' before me. It was a pattern and perhaps a rut. Life's gotten too complicated and busy for luxuries like two people meeting and sizing one another up before contracts. Besides, we both know that contracts can be easily broken if one of us is dissatisfied, no matter how ironclad those contracts appear."

With a calendar teeming full of appointments, he'd almost made a fatal mistake. He'd almost not come here and missed the opportunity of his life. "I toyed, if you'll forgive the expression, with the idea of perhaps implementing a new set of procedures. Trusting my investigators to give me the entire background on the people I deal with."

T.J. had taken out her key, but was just holding it, stunned. Christopher took it from her hand and unlocked the front door. Opening it, he waited until she crossed the threshold before following. When he gave the key back to her, she felt a jolt where his hand touched hers. It shocked her back to awareness.

He wouldn't have come and she wouldn't have

been here with him now, not being herself. T.J. didn't know whether to laugh or to cry.

The living room was dark. Only a small lamp pooled light along the hallway. Cecilia and Megan were asleep. The house was quiet.

She was alone with him, she realized. Completely alone. The thought must have occurred to him, as well. She could read that in his eyes. They were touching her, stirring her. She found the breath backing up in her throat.

"I'm glad I decided against it. They certainly were wrong in their report on you."

She tossed her head the way she'd seen Theresa do when she was flirting. Her stomach churned nervously as she hoped she hadn't overplayed her hand. How desperately she wanted what she knew she shouldn't have.

"And why is that?" The question rang husky, uttered through cotton dry lips.

Very lightly, he combed his fingers through her hair. She wore it unadorned, free, like a dark ocean beckoning him to swim in it. He watched her eyes grow large and it pleasured him.

"What they said led me to believe that you were a rather vain, rather shallow party girl who left the running of her company to very capable subordinates." Reynolds and Wagner were guilty of slacking off and letting the tabloids do their work for them. They'd been good men up to now, but he was going to have to talk to them about this when he returned. They hadn't managed to dig below the surface.

"But I'm—"

"Not," he corrected.

She couldn't spring to Theresa's defense without risking giving herself away. She wished he wouldn't look at her like that. Wouldn't touch her like that. She couldn't think when he did. And if she couldn't think, she was going to make a fatal blunder. It was only a matter of time.

"They were obviously wrong on all counts." He stood back just a little to regard her in the dim, silvery light the moon was shepherding through the bay window. "You're not vain, although there's a great deal you could be vain about. You're certainly not shallow and you've obviously worked on the presentation yourself, not left it to any subordinates to put together."

"T.J.—" The protest never managed to even leave her lips.

Loyalty, too. The tally was mounting. He couldn't help wondering why she wouldn't take credit for her own designs. "That, I think, is a smoke screen."

She shook her head. "No, she—"

Theresa was going to insist that T.J. had done the work. He might have believed her if she hadn't made that impromptu sketch.

He placed his hands on her shoulders, stilling her. "That sketch you did for me on the napkin at the restaurant… The style matched the drawings in your den."

She licked her lips, trying again. "Our styles are a lot alike—"

She'd just proved what he had surmised. Very slowly he glided the palms of his hands along her bare arms. "See, if you were vain or shallow, you'd be preening, taking the credit instead of trying to lay it on someone else's doorstep. I'm very impressed, Theresa. With the campaign.'' His eyes held her fast. ''With you.''

Her pulse quickened again as she began to feel herself turn to liquid. She wanted this, wanted this oh-so-desperately, and yet, it was dishonest. He thought—he thought—

Christopher lowered his mouth to hers and her mind joined the rest of her liquefied state.

The hell with what he thought.

T.J. fisted her hands in his thick, dark hair and gave herself to him, body and soul. She didn't think how this might make things sticky for Theresa later. She couldn't think that far ahead. Or even clearly. If she had to put up with the discomfort of pretending to be Theresa, she was damn well going to reap the rewards, just this one time. Theresa wouldn't care that he was leaving tomorrow. Theresa would be counting on it, happy not to be involved with a commitment.

Just once, she was going to see what it was like to *really* live like Theresa.

Not that she had a choice about it. And not because of him. She knew instinctively if she said no, it would stop here, in her living room. Dark, sensual, incredibly exciting, Christopher just wasn't the type to force himself on a woman.

No, the choice she didn't have was her own. She wanted this, needed this, more than she'd needed anything in a very, very long time.

The rush felt wonderful, timeless. If his hands weren't on her, she was fairly certain that she could float.

IN ANOTHER MOMENT, he thought his self-control would snap. Though he saw desire in her eyes, he wanted to be sure that this was what she wanted.

"Maybe we'd better go somewhere a little more private?" Christopher laced his hand through hers, waiting for her to demur, praying that she wouldn't. "There's this little out-of-the-way room I've been staying in that would be perfect."

It was all she could manage to nod her head. T.J. didn't even know if she smiled in response. But the rest of her was smiling. One huge grin from top to toe.

He made her feel as if she were glowing.

Christopher led her down the hallway. To her bedroom. She didn't remember walking. T.J. heard the door close behind her and the sound reverberated in her head as she looked up into his eyes.

Waiting.

Theresa wouldn't wait, she told herself. She would act.

With hands that were surprisingly steady, she undid his tie, slowly sliding the silken material down his shirtfront.

He'd never experienced anything so sensual in his life. He'd been with enough women to know. It was all he could do not to rush this. To bring it to where this pent-up feeling within him would be released.

But he didn't.

Wouldn't.

This was going to be a night to remember, for both of them. Christopher wanted their time together to stand out in her mind. He wanted to be head and shoulders above the others who had been in her life before.

There weren't, he vowed to himself, going to be any in her life hereafter. By her own choice. And for that, he was determined that he would go slow, that each moment would be burned into her brain so that there could be no room for any other men in her mind.

He would do whatever it took for her to choose him. For he had already chosen her.

It wasn't what she had expected, this lovemaking with him. It was soft, slow, liquid. Lyrical poetry. She'd never experienced agony that was sweet before. He made her ache for him with every movement, every kiss, every touch. Every tender caress. Ache for fulfillment and yet pray that it wouldn't come too soon. Not yet. She wanted this wonderful sensation of hot, palpitating anticipation to go on just a little longer.

She had no idea she could feel this way. Drugged yet excited, eager yet hesitant. Wild. He brought things out of her that she would have never believed existed. She hardly recognized herself. T.J. forgot to playact and just reacted.

Laughter bubbled and mingled with the fire in her veins.

Their clothes strewn on the floor, their limbs tangled up with each other, they left the earthly confines of her bedroom to enter a world where there was room for only two.

And that was enough.

And when it was over, when his sleek, hard body had left hers limp and glowing, he held her against him, cradling her lovingly. As if they'd always been this way. As if he'd always been her lover.

Theresa's lover, she tried to remind herself, not

hers. It didn't matter. Right now, it didn't matter. For tonight she was Theresa. Her heart was bursting with happiness and she hugged it to her.

She wanted to tell him that she had never done this before, never reacted with such intensity to a man before. Even with Peter, it had taken six months before they had made love with one another, and then only after he'd slipped an engagement ring on her finger. And that had turned out to be more promise than fulfillment.

Not this. This was something entirely new, entirely different.

But she couldn't tell him that, couldn't tell Christopher that she'd never made love with a man she hardly knew, and yet knew with all her soul. Theresa had had men in her life. He knew that. If she said anything, he'd laugh at her. Or think she was lying. Her mouth twisted. Ironic, wasn't it?

Yet she desperately wanted to tell him something. Wanted him to know how special this was for her. How wonderfully different.

The words came without preamble. "I've never done this before."

Propping himself on his elbow, he raised a quizzical brow. He could feel her hair feathering along his chest as she picked up her head to look at him.

"Made love to a client."

He didn't know if he believed her. He knew he wanted to. "Then I guess this makes me your first." He'd settle for that, he thought. For now. Bowing his head, he brushed his lips against hers.

The combustion was instantaneous. The fire roared hotter than before.

THE TELEPHONE ROUSED HER. The jangling noise intruded into her dreams, breaking them up like so many soap bubbles in a sink.

When she managed to open her eyes a crack, she saw that light was flooding the room. Morning. How had it come so quickly?

The noise persisted. The phone—she had to answer the phone.

As she groped for the receiver, T.J. realized that she wasn't alone. There was a warm body next to hers. A nude warm body.

Christopher.

Last night.

This morning.

Oh, God!

T.J. jerked into wakefulness as she simultaneously glanced over her shoulder to see if he was still asleep and rasped a "hello" into the receiver.

"T.J.?" Theresa's voice, far too exhilarated, filled her ear.

Christopher was stirring beside her. The telephone had woken him up. T.J. turned her body away from him, gathering the sheet to her as she lowered her voice.

"Yes?"

"T.J., it's Theresa." This time, she sounded puzzled. "I'm finally home. Just got in this morning. The resident doctor wanted to check me out himself." She laughed, the sound pregnant and familiar. "I'm seeing him again tonight, So, how did it go Friday?"

"Fine." The response was terse. She hoped that Theresa would take the hint and hang up.

Luck wasn't with her. All she had managed to do

was rouse Theresa's curiosity. "Why are you whispering? Is something wrong?"

"I'll explain later," T.J. whispered. Theresa had certainly received enough inopportune phone calls herself to know when someone else wanted to get off. Why wasn't she taking the hint?

T.J. felt Christopher's hand on her bare shoulder and nearly groaned as his fingers lightly skimmed along her skin. She knew she squirmed as memories of their lovemaking haunted her body.

Theresa sounded as if she wanted to settle in for a chat. "No, tell me now. Did MacAffee like what you had to show him?"

The man in question cupped her breast, teasing the end with his thumb. T.J. sucked in her breath. The words were tight when she spoke. "I think so."

"Are you all right?" Theresa repeated. "You sound funny."

"I'm fine, just fine. I'll get back to you later, Th— T.J." Biting the tip of her tongue, T.J. broke off the conversation. That had been close.

"T.J.?" Theresa's voice echoed as T.J. hung up the telephone.

Suddenly she found herself being turned around until she was flat on her back, gazing up into the greenest eyes God ever created.

"That was T.J.," she murmured.

He began to nibble at her neck, loving the way she twisted beneath him. Excitement pulsed through his loins in anticipation.

"So I gathered."

T.J. could feel the words along her throat. She arched, wanting to feel more. To feel him.

"She seems very conscientious, calling you on a Sunday."

T.J. swallowed before she could continue. "You don't know the half of it." She tried to muster some strength. There wasn't much to spare and what there was, she had a hunch, she was going to need soon. "So, what do you want for breakfast?"

He raised his head to look at her, his eyes teasing. "You."

Once more with feeling, she thought, happiness spreading like golden marmalade all through her. T.J. twined her arms around his neck, bringing him closer to her. "One serving, over easy, coming up."

It was the last thing either one of them said for a while.

"ABOUT TIME THE TWO OF YOU showed up for breakfast." Cecilia raised her brows, amused, in Christopher's direction. "I see you got your strength back." She made no effort to hide her knowing grin as she placed a plate of French toast before each of them on the table. She grinned at Christopher before turning to T.J. "I am taking Megan to the park in case you would like to continue those undercover negotiations you were conducting."

Certainly wasn't shy about things, was she? "How did you know?" he asked the woman. They hadn't made any noise. And the hour had been sufficiently late when they returned. He'd assumed the housekeeper had been asleep.

"Cecilia likes to think she knows everything. She makes good guesses." T.J. looked at Cecilia pointedly. "But not this time."

T.J. could see it in the other woman's eyes. Cecilia was thinking, *Yeah, right.* T.J. pressed on. What she'd shared with him had been exquisite, but now it was over and she had to come to terms with that.

"There aren't going to be any more negotiations," T.J. told her. She deliberately avoided Cecilia's eyes. "We seemed to have settled everything to both our satisfaction." The housekeeper was chuckling to herself. T.J. looked at Christopher. "What time do you want Emmett here to take you to the airport?"

"Oh, didn't I tell you?" Christopher smiled at her. He knew perfectly well that he hadn't. It was a surprise. One he'd just come up with. He'd made the necessary arrangements while she'd been in the shower. "I've decided to stay around for a few more days."

T.J. dropped her fork.

8

T.J. QUICKLY PICKED UP her fork again. She stared at the man sitting across from her at the kitchen table. The man who had made her body sing.

The man who had to leave before he found out he had made love to the wrong woman.

T.J. had to clear her throat twice before she could speak. "Excuse me?"

He'd hoped for a slightly less violent reaction. "I've decided to remain here for a few more days."

To be here with you. He almost said it out loud, but stopped himself. It would sound absurd for him to have developed such strong feelings for her so quickly. And maybe it was. He had to find out.

"But why—?"

He thought she'd be more pleased. It disturbed him that she looked as if she was in shock. "I want to come down to the office with you. Kick off the Valentine's Day campaign."

That was only partially true. It had come out of nowhere this morning, hitting him with the impact of a detonating six-megaton bomb. Christopher wanted to be part of all the other facets of her life. He savored the rush this new feeling created. Like Christmas Day when his mother had still been part of his life. He couldn't remember details, only a feeling. If he concentrated very hard, he could remember an aura of happiness surrounding him. He'd felt contented then.

Just the way he felt now.

She was the woman for him. He could feel it. But years of caution couldn't be readily ignored or dismissed. It wasn't in his nature. He had to spend a little more time with Theresa before he said anything to her about the way he felt. Although, if she was as intuitive as he thought, words weren't going to be necessary.

And it wouldn't hurt to lay a little groundwork for himself while he was at it, either. Just because things came easily to him, Christopher wasn't so naive or so pompous as to believe that the lady would just fall into his arms. Not even after a night of incredible lovemaking. There had been other men in her life, even if casually. There probably still were now. He wanted to create a situation in which Theresa Cochran would do some voluntary house cleaning on her own.

"The office?" she repeated dumbly, still staring at him. A numbness washed over her before panic set in. Her mind began to scramble, searching for alternatives. "But I thought you had to be getting back."

The noise behind her told her Cecilia was still in the room, listening. She glanced at the woman over her shoulder, silently asking for help. The look in Cecilia's eyes told her that there wasn't going to be any coming from that quarter. Cecilia was amused by this turn of events. But then, Cecilia would have matched her up with the mailman if the man had stayed around longer than just to deliver the mail.

Feeling like the activities coordinator on the *Ti-*

tanic, T.J. turned around to look at Christopher again. He *had* to be kidding.

"I do have to get back."

T.J. almost breathed a sigh of relief, but it would have been wasted in light of what Christopher said next.

"But I called Abrams," he said, naming a vice president she'd dealt with herself when she'd called the main office, "while you were showering. Told him I was going to be detained for a few days overseeing the new advertising campaign."

How many days in "a few"? T.J. wondered, fragments of thoughts floating through her mind like so much driftwood as panic grew.

"I think I'll be leaving now," Cecilia announced. She draped her apron over the back of a chair. "Looks like a good day for playing to me." She winked at T.J.

T.J. glared at the retreating back as Cecilia went to find Megan.

She was usually so creative when she was staring at a blank piece of paper or a pristine computer screen. Why was her mind turning to mush now, damn it, when she needed it most?

The excuse that rose to her lips was a lame one at best. "Well, we usually work best without someone looking over our shoulder."

She was acting almost shy, he thought, bemused. Why? Maybe he was just being overly sensitive. Small wonder—he'd never gone out on a limb this way before.

With the appetite of someone who was starving, he

began to make short work of his French toast. "I won't get in the way," he promised.

If you only knew.

Okay, he was staying. She had to work with that. Gathering her wits together, T.J. began to mount a defensive. There were things that had to be done if they were going to get away with this. Placing her hands on the table, she began to push herself away.

"All right, let me make some calls of my own about this."

He caught her wrist before she could stand up. "But it's Sunday." Even he didn't work on Sunday. Usually.

Very carefully, she reclaimed her wrist. "Your vice president isn't the only one on call Sundays." She tried to make her voice sound casual. It wasn't easy with her heart and stomach both lodged in her throat. "Here." She pushed her untouched plate toward him. His was nearly empty. "Have mine. I don't really eat much in the morning."

Which was a lie. She always woke up hungry and enjoyed having a huge breakfast. But this morning, she wouldn't have been able to sneak a bite past her lips. Not when her insides were lurching like this.

Leaving Christopher to eat, T.J. went straight to the den. Cecilia and Megan were preparing to go out. T.J. gave her daughter a quick hug and a kiss before she left. As the front door closed, T.J. breathed a quick sigh of relief. One less worry, at least for the time being.

Two million to go. Shaking her head, she locked herself in the small room. She didn't want to be overheard.

Her hand was shaking as she tapped out the familiar numbers on the keypad. She wished she could just sit back and enjoy this instead of trying to reconnoiter and head off this latest turn of events.

Why did everything involving Theresa always have to be so complicated?

Theresa's answering machine came on after four rings. Impatiently, T.J. listened to the low, sultry voice on the other end apologize for being unable to reach the telephone. "Leave a message and I *will* get back to you."

Was it just her, or did that almost sound like an obscene promise?

"C'mon, c'mon. Pick up. Pick up, Theresa, I know you're there." Her teeth were clenched as she ordered, "Pick up the damn telephone."

Just as she was about to give up and leave a message, T.J. heard the receiver on the other end being lifted from the cradle.

"I knew there was something wrong," Theresa told her, not even bothering to say hello. "We lost the account, didn't we? He saw right through you and knew you weren't me. Oh, God, T.J. if you weren't such a mouse—"

She didn't have much time. Christopher was going to come looking for her soon. T.J. cut through the rest of Theresa's lecture, one she knew by heart. Theresa was always after her to change, to kick up her heels and follow her example.

Well, she had, and now look at the trouble they were all in.

"Theresa, you can't come into the office tomorrow."

The request took her completely by surprise. "Why?"

Feeling as if all the air had suddenly been drained out of her, T.J. sighed as she sagged against the chair. "Because Christopher is. He wants to look around, see where I—where *you* work."

"Christopher?"

T.J. drummed her fingers on the desk impatiently. Didn't Theresa ever do her homework? She was sharper than this. T.J. *knew* she was.

"MacAffee." T.J.'s clenched jaw was beginning to ache. "He's decided to stay over a few days and see how we operate."

"Why? I thought you said he was satisfied with your performance."

Theresa didn't sound nearly as distressed as T.J. thought she'd be. Definitely not as distressed as she was. Probably because her cousin figured she could handle this. Well she didn't think she could. Not this time. It was like trying to juggle with torches that had been set on fire. Sooner or later, she was going to get burned.

"He is." T.J. dragged her hand through her hair. "Maybe too much." A germ of an idea took seed. It was their only chance. "Listen, I don't have time to give you all the details now—" *Not that I ever would.* "But don't be there tomorrow. No, wait, you do have to be there tomorrow," she realized. "You have to tell everyone to pretend that I'm you. At least the head staff." T.J. began scribbling notes to herself on the pad. There was so much to remember. "Oh God, Theresa, this is turning out to be such a mess."

Theresa sounded completely unruffled. "We'll get through this. I've got a lot of faith in you."

Easy for you to say. You don't have to face him. "I really don't like lying to the man like this."

The laugh was light, amused and perhaps just the slightest bit patronizing. "Once you start, T.J., it's easy."

"If you say so. Oh, by the way." About to hang up, she remembered what would have been the most important part—if last night hadn't happened. "We've got to get started on a Valentine's Day campaign for MacAffee Toys."

"This Valentine's Day?"

Even in the midst of the storm, a flicker of satisfaction went through her. "Yes."

There was a genuine note of admiration. "Boy, you do work fast."

More than you know, cousin, more than you'll ever know. T.J. rose from the desk. She had to get back. "All right, I have to go now. I left Christopher in the kitchen and he might start to wonder what happened to me."

"The kitchen?" Theresa echoed. "What's MacAffee doing in your house?"

"A long, long story. It starts out with a virus."

"Computer?"

"Human. Bye."

T.J. hung up, then spared a satisfied look at the telephone. She'd deliberately left Theresa hanging and she had to admit it felt good just once to turn the tables on her cousin.

Maybe she had wanted this more than she'd admitted to herself, T.J. thought, unlocking the door. Otherwise, why would it feel so good?

She had no time to dwell on that. She had to come up with a plan to fall back on.

And she didn't have an idea in her head.

Nothing had occurred to her by the time she walked into the kitchen. She was just going to have to play this by ear and pray things worked out.

Man, but he was gorgeous, she thought as she approached Christopher. If Theresa had known what he looked like, she would have found a way to get to the airport, even if it meant having her hospital bed transported with her.

Christopher threaded an arm around her waist and pulled her onto his lap. "Missed you."

She tasted honey on his lips when he kissed her. Or was that just him? She could really get used to this, she mused. Too bad she was never going to get the chance.

He could smell the shampoo she'd used. Something herbal. Who would have thought herbs could be sensual? "How long does Cecilia usually take when she brings Megan to the park?"

Her hands seemed to have a mind of their own as they wound themselves around his neck. "Oh, I don't know. A couple of hours. Maybe more."

It was just what he wanted to hear. "Good, that gives us some time."

Anticipation began to nudge forward. She squelched it. He probably wasn't talking about what she was hoping he was talking about. "Time?"

"Well, I'm going to check into a hotel this afternoon." He couldn't remain here. It wasn't proper.

Besides, it would give them somewhere private to go without having to worry about the housekeeper. "I imagine the conventions are over by this afternoon." He saw the surprise in her eyes. "I don't want to compromise your reputation."

Now *there* was a first, she thought. Someone actually worried about Theresa's reputation. It certainly didn't bother Theresa. Gossip just rolled off her back.

But he really wasn't talking about Theresa's reputation, T.J. thought. He was talking about hers. Never mind that he thought it was one and the same. She took it for what it was: a chivalrous act.

"Very noble of you."

"But before I leave..." He pressed a kiss to her throat and felt her sigh. "I thought that perhaps we could review some familiar ground."

T.J. melted against him, done in by the look in his eyes. She'd never seen anything so tender, so loving.

She damned Theresa and blessed her in the same breath as he kissed her again. If not for Theresa, she wouldn't have been able to sample heaven. And if not for Theresa, she wouldn't have to relinquish it again.

His mouth still sealed to hers, Christopher rose with her in his arms. He carried T.J. to her bedroom where they did indeed cover familiar ground. And make it new all over again.

PERPETUALLY TENSE, T.J. felt like a soldier picking his way through a mine field. The only time she felt at ease was when the door was shut and there was just the two of them in a room. At least then, she only had to worry about tripping herself up and not about anyone else accidentally addressing her as T.J. or making some sort of other slip.

In the few days that she'd been showing Christopher around the office, she had been a nervous wreck. Dressed in the suits Theresa had covertly sent over via her maid, T.J. did her best to play the role of the flamboyant company president.

She'd taken to the part so well that after a while, people were hard-pressed to tell her apart from the original. T.J. had overheard Heidi tell one of the secretaries in the pool that she looked more like Theresa than Theresa did.

She just acted a little differently, Heidi had gone on to say. More savvy, and, it turned out, more daring when it came to business.

By the end of the third day, T.J. finally began to relax a little. Giving orders actually came easily to her. She was on familiar ground. She'd been on both sides of the drawing board.

It was going to turn out all right, T.J. assured herself. At least, as far as business was concerned. The rest of the problem was another matter entirely. But she couldn't think about that now, not in the middle of her charade. There was just too much to do, too many torches to keep in the air at the same time. So far, she hadn't gotten burned.

And when Christopher was around her, in the privacy of his suite, she couldn't think at all. She didn't want to. All she wanted to do was feel. To store up every delicious sensation, every wondrous moment for a lifetime. Because she knew it was going to end all too soon.

The nights they spent together were as exquisite as

a flawlessly cut diamond placed in a perfect setting. It wasn't just the lovemaking, which only seemed to grow more magnificent with practice. It was more.

It was the little things. Like standing on his balcony and looking up at the stars, so high above the city, so close to them that she thought she could just reach up and touch one. Like sipping champagne from the same glass, with their eyes on one another. Or like holding one another in the afterglow of lovemaking and feeling his heart beat beneath her cheek.

All little things. All precious.

She was hopelessly in love with the man and there was nothing she could do about it. Only enjoy the tiny moment in time she'd been granted.

T.J. managed to get away a few times and touched base with Megan. Gratefully, the little girl was none the worse for the separation. Because she did travel, her daughter was accustomed to not seeing her on a daily basis. T.J. knew she had to pack a lifetime into the short stay. But as the days whirled by, she was getting the very clear impression that it wasn't going to be over once he boarded the plane.

Heaven knew she didn't want it to be. But how could it continue? If he came back, he was going to have to be told the truth. And then what? What man could laugh off being deceived?

He would never trust her again.

The thought brought a pang to her heart, even as she lay curled beside him in the hotel suite bed.

Drawing her even closer to him, Christopher pressed a kiss to her forehead. These last few days had been incredible. He felt alive for perhaps the first time in his life. He was grateful to her for that, for opening his eyes to this brave new world.

She was a dynamo in the office. And even more so in bed. He was damn lucky to have found her.

The sigh that escaped her lips lingered over his chest. "A penny for your thoughts?"

There was no way she was going to volunteer that. T.J. forced herself to smile. "Only a penny?" she teased. "Is that how you managed to make your fortune? Underpaying people?"

He laughed. "The fortune, as you call it, was made long before I came into the picture. I just pulled the company a little further into the twentieth century, that's all."

She brushed aside the one wayward lock of hair that fell into his eyes, trying not to think about how much she was going to miss him. "I think you're going to have to push a little harder. We're approaching the twenty-*first,* you know."

"No hurry." It was hard deciding which flavor he enjoyed most. The one at her neck, the one behind her elbow. The one he'd discovered behind her knee. He enjoyed sampling and trying to make a choice. "I figure we'll make that transition in about another fifty years. There'll be another MacAffee at the helm by then and it won't be my concern. What I'm concerned with," he told her as he forged a slow, sensuous hot trail along her body, "is the here and now." He raised his head, his eyes on hers. "And you."

He was looking at her as if she was something precious, and she felt like such a fraud. Her body, so fresh from lovemaking, was heating again. It always would. To his touch.

"You always get so caught up in your work?"

"Never." The affirmation skimmed along her taut belly, making it tighten. "I didn't know what I was missing." The kisses were becoming more ardent, making it harder for her to form a coherent thought.

No, not harder. Impossible.

Christopher raised himself on his elbows, looking down into her face. He didn't like what he was about to say. "I'm going to have to leave tomorrow."

She knew that. Had known that. It was what she'd planned on.

The sinking sensation she felt was almost unbearable. "Tomorrow?"

He liked the echo of loneliness he heard in her voice. It matched his own.

"I have to. Everyone at the company thinks I must have lost my mind." His mouth curved. "I've never taken time off before."

She held him then, as if having her arms around him formed a magic circle where no harm could come to either of them. And the truth stood just outside. "Never?"

He shook his head, his body curving into hers. Savoring it. "Not more than a day or two. I love my work. It reaffirms me. Maybe it even defines me. Or did," he amended with a fond smile as he gazed at her. "I hadn't realized just how nice it was to 'kick back.' Those were the words you used, weren't they?"

She wouldn't have been able to swear to anything right now. "Sounds like me."

He had an inspiration. "Come up with me," Christopher proposed suddenly. "Fly up to San Jose. I'll return the favor and show you around."

She was tempted. Tempted to continue the charade just a little longer. What would it hurt?

Everything.

With more regret than she had thought there was in the world, she shook her head. "I can't. We're launching your campaign Monday, remember?"

It hadn't been easy. The whole company had dropped everything to mount this television commercial. Buying a time slot so close to the holiday had been almost impossible. But Theresa had put in a few phone calls, pulled in a favor and a prime thirty-second opening on the most popular sitcom on the airwaves came their way. Once that was known, several others had materialized. The price tag had been hefty, but the returns, T.J. was certain, were going to be tremendous.

Her parting gift to Christopher, she thought sadly.

He frowned slightly. "You don't have to be here to do that."

"Yes, I do," she contradicted. And it was true. She did have to be here. It was her baby to oversee. "It's more complicated than you think."

"Can't you give it to T.J. to do?" he suggested. "I still haven't met her, you know." She'd promised to introduce him to her cousin, but each time he brought it up, the woman was elusively missing.

Yes, you have. I'm right here, in your arms. "She's been very busy this past week."

He shrugged, not really interested in anyone else. Only Theresa. He'd asked to meet the woman only because T.J. was related to Theresa and Theresa seemed to think so highly of her. The only person he wanted to see was right here, in his bed.

"There's time for that later." The meeting was already forgotten. There was something far more pressing on his mind. "Are you sure I can't convince you to come with me?"

She wanted to say yes. No one knew who she was at his company. But that would only be drawing a host of others into the deception. Others who might hold it against Christopher for some reason. She couldn't do that to him. "I'm sure."

He blew out a breath, disappointed. And then he smiled, shifting over her. "Well, then I guess I just have to make the most of the time I have, don't I?"

She couldn't go on this way. The burden of the lie was killing her. "Christopher, I have something to tell you."

He didn't like the look in her eyes. It had to do with them. He could sense it. He didn't want to hear her say something like this past week had been fun, but that now it was over. He didn't want it to be over. And he was going to do his damnedest to make her not want it to be over, either.

"Shhh." He pressed a kiss to first one temple, then the other. "I don't want to talk about business right now."

"This isn't about business."

The words were getting harder and harder to get out. He was kissing the hollow of her throat and tears sprang to her eyes. Tears of joy, of regret. This would be the last time, she promised herself, the last time she'd let him make love to someone she wasn't.

The last time.

She was going to make the most of it.

He thought he knew her. Knew what she was capable of. He didn't know a thing. The woman in his bed became a whirlwind of passion. A tigress. He had always been the one to take the initiative, to lead the way. Now the reins, it seemed, had passed into her hands. He surrendered them willingly.

When she rolled over and pushed him onto his back, pleasuring him in ways he'd never even dreamed, he became weak as a kitten. It wasn't a role he would have thought he'd enjoy.

But then he'd already realized that he didn't know a damned thing.

She reduced him to a mass of wanting, of ignited passion that seemed to know no end, no resolution. Her fingers lightly glided along his body, kneading, touching, possessing, sculpting. Taking his breath away as he realized the depths to which his desire extended.

"Where," he breathed, hating the man who had taught her this even as he was grateful to him, "did you learn to do this?"

"Instinct," she whispered raggedly against his ear. "Pure instinct."

She couldn't have given him a better gift if she'd tried.

9

HE'D BEEN IN and out of airports all of his life, flying away to boarding school, then home for holidays. Away on business. They all blurred in his mind. Christopher couldn't really remember a single instance clearly.

This time, he knew, he would remember. He would remember the way he felt right now, standing here with Theresa saying goodbye, until the day he died—no matter what came after.

Christopher looked down into her upturned face. He could have been standing in the middle of a "Star Trek" convention and he wouldn't have noticed anyone else but her.

The loudspeaker squawked as the announcement came to an end. They were calling for final boarding of his flight.

He didn't want to leave.

One last time, he lost himself in her eyes, in the dimple that winked at the corner of her mouth as she smiled at him.

It was a sad smile and they shared it.

Standing near the entrance of the boarding ramp that funneled its way into the airplane, Christopher leaned his head against hers and sighed.

"You know, I caught myself wishing that I'd miss

this flight. Where are those famous L.A. traffic jams they're always talking about when you need them?"

The same thing had occurred to her. And the same wish. But Emmett had had almost a clear path from the house to LAX. It was as if some unforeseen hand had moved aside all the excess vehicles, sweeping them away.

The flight attendant at the entrance cleared her throat, waiting. Urgency hummed in T.J.'s veins. This was going to be the last time she saw him like this. The last time, in all probability, that she saw him at all. It had to be.

"That was pretty much of a miracle, wasn't it? Maybe it's a sign that you should go back." *I don't want you to leave. I don't want this to end. Most of all, I don't want you to ever find out that I lied to you.*

But he would, she thought, a fathomless sadness filling her. He would. And then…

There was something in her eyes, a depth of sadness that spoke to him. She didn't want him to leave any more than he wanted to go. There should be a way around this. But for now he knew there wasn't. He couldn't forsake the businessman in him entirely, even though for the first time in his life he desperately wanted to.

Christopher framed her face with his hands. These last few days had been indescribably incredible. He felt almost as if he were being struck by lightning. Or born for the very first time. Strange sensation to relish at the age of thirty-three. He wasn't about to relinquish what he'd just found. This separation, Christopher promised himself, was just temporary.

"I only read the signs I like," he assured her with a grin.

You won't like any of this, once you know the truth. She glanced over her shoulder at the flight attendant. There was understanding in the blond woman's eyes as she gestured them forward. There was a time schedule to adhere to, love notwithstanding.

T.J. slipped her arms around his neck. One kiss, one last kiss. "If you don't hurry, you're going to miss your flight."

Would that be so bad? he wondered. There'd be another one in its place. But there were things he had to attend to. He couldn't just shrug off responsibilities because his insides felt as if they'd been drop-kicked by a mule. Or just because he found himself lost in a beautiful woman's eyes.

Ignoring the attendant's light touch on his arm, Christopher kissed T.J. Long and hard, with the passion of someone going away for a very long time, instead of the week he silently planned.

"Sir."

He broke contact and began to back away down the ramp, still looking at T.J. "I'll send one of my people down with the contracts as soon as they're signed."

To make their mutual lawyers happy, he'd signed a temporary agreement so that C & C Advertising could get the Valentine's Day commercial underway, but a ream of legal documents were waiting for his signature before the deal was final.

T.J. watched as the distance between them lengthened. The sadness within her grew in direct geometric proportions. "I'll be waiting for them."

At the last moment, just before he would have disappeared around the corner and into the plane, Christopher sprinted back up the ramp. The attendant, taken by surprise, didn't follow immediately. When she did, she was exasperated.

"Sir—"

He didn't bother to turn around. He wanted to keep looking at the woman who had brought rainbows into his world. "Just another minute."

Frazzled, the attendant looked over her shoulder at another woman who emerged from the far end of the ramp near the plane. She shrugged at her helplessly. "But the flight—"

There wasn't time for anything more than a fleeting kiss. It wouldn't be fair to keep a whole plane waiting. Releasing her, he hurried back down.

"Valentine's Day," he called out to T.J.

She didn't understand. Was he telling her something about the TV campaign? "What?"

"I'll be back for Valentine's Day," he promised, raising his voice above the noise emerging from the end of the ramp. "Keep it open."

And with that, he disappeared into the waiting airplane and out of her life.

"Goodbye," T.J. whispered.

She stood there, immobile, even when the attendant returned to close the door. The woman flashed her a sympathetic look.

T.J. was vaguely aware of the attendant nodding at her. She stepped back, lost in a sea of emotion. Relief and misery joined hands in an awkward minuet. She was relieved Christopher was finally on the plane and the danger of exposure was temporarily over. And yet she was so miserable, she felt she could curl up and die.

Valentine's Day.

He said he'd be back on Valentine's Day. Ironic, wasn't it? She'd always wanted someone to make a fuss over her on Valentine's Day. Theresa had always been the one inundated with gifts and dates. No one had even thought to send her a card.

Not even Peter. She'd met him in late February, just after Valentine's had passed. By the time the holiday had rolled around again, they were together, but he was so complacent in their relationship, he hadn't bothered to even take note of Valentine's Day.

A sad smile curved her lips. She'd always strongly identified with Charlie Brown and the empty mailbox, knowing just how he felt.

And now, with a promise of romance lingering fresh in the air, she still couldn't look forward to the day. Because she didn't want him returning. Didn't want him ever finding out that she had deceived him. And he would if he came back. How long could her luck hold out? How long could she keep up the charade?

Taking the escalator down to street level, she let her mind drift in a momentary fantasy. Christopher and she celebrating their fiftieth anniversary in an exclusive restaurant, surrounded by children and grandchildren. Her hand would be on his, about to cut the five-foot-high cake. A tiny replica of them the way they'd been on their wedding day would stand on the top tier.

''Um, honey, there's something I have to tell you,''

she would whisper in his ear. *"I'm really my cousin T.J. and Megan is really my daughter."*

And then Christopher would drop the knife and walk out of the restaurant. Out of her life forever.

She wasn't even able to make him understand in her fantasy. She certainly couldn't hope to find the right words in real life.

Maybe she wouldn't have to.

The prospect didn't cheer her.

T.J. walked out of the terminal, looking for Emmett and the black stretch limo.

Odds were that once Christopher was back in San Jose, concerns about business would swallow him up and he'd forget he'd ever said anything. After all, men took these liaisons lightly.

But she didn't.

She blinked back tears as she saw the car and began walking to it.

Just as well if he didn't come back.

The hell it was.

Emmett sprang to attention when he saw her, tucking the newspaper he'd been reading under his arm. One look at her face and he felt his heartstrings being tugged.

"You certainly look down-and-out." Moving nimbly, Emmett opened the rear door for her. He made a guess. "Mr. MacAffee find out at the last minute?"

T.J. shook her head. The interior of the car looked too lonely for her to bear. "Mind if I ride up front with you?" She turned her moist eyes to his and hoped he wouldn't notice that she'd been trying not to cry. "I could use the company."

Emmett offered her his handkerchief. She took it

and dried her eyes. Of all the people he had ever driven around, Mr. Shawn's daughter had been the only one who had ever related to him on an equal footing. He thought the world of her and hated seeing her so unhappy.

"My pleasure, miss." He opened the front door for her before she could reach for it.

Rounding the hood, Emmett took his seat quickly and started the limousine. Expertly, he maneuvered the large automobile as if it was no more than a VW Bug, weaving in and out of traffic. Taking Century Boulevard, he entered the freeway.

Emmett decided to hazard one last guess, hoping he was right. He didn't want to think of her crying over a man. "Contract fall through?"

"No, the contract's fine." Theresa, at least, would be very happy. "Which is more than I can say for me," she whispered under her breath.

Making no comment, Emmett reached over to the radio. He turned the knob until he found what he was looking for. An oldies station.

T.J. looked at him in surprise, then smiled. Emmett hated oldies music with a passion. All he ever listened to was classical. But he knew she liked it.

"Thanks."

He nodded. "Don't mention it."

She sat back, staring straight ahead, trying to sort things out in her mind. She couldn't, not yet. "They're right about what they say."

"And what's that, miss?" His voice was soothing, low-key.

"About what a tangled web we weave when first

we practice to deceive.'' It was more than something in a dusty book of quotations. It was now her life.

"Wouldn't know about that, miss. My life's very untangled."

She laughed softly. "You don't know how lucky you are, Emmett."

His small brown eyes met hers as he stopped the car at the light. "Oh, I don't know. Sometimes I would have welcomed a bit of a tangle." He gave her an encouraging smile. "Things have a habit of working themselves out. Wait and see."

Not this time, she thought. But she only nodded in response. There was no sense in discussing it. What was done was done.

THERESA WAS THE FIRST one in her path when she got off the elevator an hour later. T.J. had come to the office straight from the airport. Maybe if she kept busy enough, she just wouldn't think.

It was a feeble plan at best, doomed to failure.

Theresa was dressed in the subdued fashion T.J. always favored, her bountiful hair pulled back just the way T.J. wore hers when she came to work. Though she hadn't run into Christopher by design, Theresa had thought it prudent, though annoying, to dress the part she had reluctantly assumed until the man returned up north. Just in case.

She looked eagerly behind T.J. as the latter walked out of the elevator. There was no one with her. Theresa turned bright, hopeful eyes on her cousin. "Well, did you get him off?"

T.J. nodded. Never breaking stride, she continued walking down the hall to her office.

"Thank God!" With a dramatic sigh, Theresa pulled the clip from her hair and tossed her head. Her dark hair rained about her shoulders. "I can be me again." She shoved the clip into T.J.'s hands. "I didn't think I could stand this masquerade much longer." Combing her fingers through her hair, she followed T.J. down the hall, absently wondering what the hurry was. "You know, you really got the better end of the deal." She turned toward her own office and the change of clothes she'd brought in in the hope that they'd seen the last of Christopher MacAffee at the office. Theresa twisted a button open on her blouse. "I don't know how you can stand these drab clothes."

"They're comfortable," T.J. answered absently. Without thinking about it, she drew her hair back and caught it in the clip.

"They're awful." Theresa stopped and looked at T.J. She didn't look like a woman who had successfully driven home a major deal. "Are you all right? Anything wrong with the deal?"

The deal. The word echoed in T.J.'s brain. That was all that mattered. People, whole families, depended on their landing large accounts. And MacAffee Toys was a big one. She had to keep that in mind.

"The deal is alive and well. He's sending the final contracts back down via a courier as soon as they're signed."

"Good job." Pleased, Theresa hugged T.J. T.J. wasn't hugging back. T.J. always hugged back. Puzzled, Theresa peered at her face. T.J. turned away and walked into her office. Concerned, Theresa followed.

"There is something wrong." She knew it was too easy. There was a catch to the agreement. "What?"

When was this hollow feeling going to let go of her? Her back to Theresa, T.J. squeezed her eyes shut to hold back the tears. "What could be wrong? We have a multimillion-dollar company on our books and an inspired commercial on the air, which the head of the company thinks is charming. Everything's wonderful. Couldn't be better."

Sarcasm wasn't T.J.'s long suit. Theresa became sincerely worried. But when she touched her cousin's shoulder, T.J. shrugged her away.

"T.J.—"

The last thing she wanted was to talk about it. Or worse, see pity in Theresa's eyes. "If you don't mind, I think I'll get out of these clothes and get some work done, all right?"

She knew when she was being dismissed. For once, Theresa let it slide. T.J. wasn't one to discuss her problems. Unlike her.

Reluctantly, Theresa obliged her and backed out of the office. "Maybe we can go out to lunch later?"

"Right," T.J. muttered to herself as she heard the door close. "We'll do lunch."

She stared out the window at the perfect day outside. She wished it would rain.

HE SUPPOSED HE WAS behaving like some lovesick adolescent, but Christopher figured he owed it to himself. He'd entirely skipped that portion of his life the first time around. He selected the next taxi queued up to the curb in front of the terminal and tossed his bag into the back seat.

"11737 Wilshire," he said in answer to the driver's raised brow.

The man nodded as he got into the cab.

Christopher looked out the window at the crowded lot, anxious to be there already. To see the look of surprise in Theresa's eyes when he walked into her office.

Yes, he mused, just like an adolescent. Or so he surmised. There had never been a girl in his teens he'd been smitten with. He'd been too busy being groomed for his position in the firm, constantly being reminded that the company, and its fate, would all rest on his shoulders someday. He was not to disappoint the generation that had come before. That hadn't left a hell of a lot of room or time for anything else.

And he wasn't exactly smitten now. At least, not only that. He was smitten, infatuated and head over heels. The whole gamut, up to and including wildly in love.

A horn blared behind them and the cabdriver muttered something in a foreign tongue that obviously wasn't very flattering. Christopher hardly heard him. His mind was elsewhere.

This was it—the woman he wanted to marry. He knew himself well enough to know that though this appeared like a snap judgment on his part, it wasn't. It was very sound.

He liked everything about her. Playing his own devil's advocate, he had tried to find a flaw, something to pick at, and couldn't. For a whole week, he'd tried, thinking that being away from her would naturally cool any fire he had felt.

It only fanned it.

The entire time he had been away from her, he'd been preoccupied. Snippets of the moments they'd spent together would replay themselves through his mind and he would drift off in the middle of meetings. People began to notice and to talk. This was completely out of character for him. It was chalked up as something to do with his recent illness.

Well, if this was being ill, he hoped he'd never get well.

Christopher looked down at the envelope on the cracked vinyl seat beside him. On impulse, he'd decided to bring the contracts back down himself rather than send them by courier, or Express Mail. He had never done anything on impulse before. But he wanted an excuse to see her again; he *needed* to see her again.

Like a kid, he thought with a grin. A kid who knew what he wanted.

More horns blared. He felt his impatience mounting. Christopher slid forward, leaning toward the driver. "Can't this thing go any faster?"

The driver snorted, waving a dismissive hand at the cars around them. "It could, if the traffic was moving, which, if you look, it ain't." Dark shaggy brows drooped over penetrating, black marble eyes as he looked over his shoulder at his fare. "Take it easy, mister. I'm doing the best I can. Whoever you're seeing'll still be there by the time I get you to Wilshire."

True enough, but it didn't dissipate the sense of urgency he felt. "I've wasted thirty-three years. I don't want to waste any more."

The driver just shrugged in response, turning forward again. Tourists. They were all the same. Crazy and in a hurry to get there.

CHRISTOPHER RELISHED the fact that his behavior was completely out of character for him. Normally, he would have had his assistant call her assistant and arrange a meeting. But that was before he'd met her. Now he couldn't wait to see the look on her face. Couldn't wait to touch that face, to hold her against him.

God, but he had missed her.

Getting off on the seventh floor, he hurried down the corridor to Theresa's office.

Heidi's myopic eyes were round as Frisbees as she recognized him. Jumping to her feet, the word *Mayday* flashed through her mind.

"Sir, wait. You can't go in there. She's in conference." It was the first thing that popped into her head.

"I won't say a word until she's finished," he promised, passing Heidi's desk. Knocking once, he opened the door to Theresa's office and then walked in, whistling.

In the middle of a call, her chair turned toward the window, Theresa heard the door to her office open and close. Heidi usually buzzed her before entering. Bemused, Theresa turned her chair around to face the door.

There was an incredibly good-looking man standing in her office. Well, well, well, Valentine's Day had arrived early this year.

"I'll call you back," Theresa murmured into the receiver, her eyes never leaving the stranger. She hung up before the person on the other end had a chance to respond.

A broad, inviting smile of welcome spread out over her lips.

The smile on Christopher's faded slightly as he stepped forward. He had the oddest feeling....

"Theresa?"

"Yes?"

He obviously had an advantage over her, she thought. But that wouldn't be for long. She intended to have one over him before the evening ended.

Christopher shook his head. Something was out of kilter. There was something about her.... "No."

Theresa blinked. "Excuse me?"

"You're not." He moved closer, looking at her. Studying her. She looked like Theresa, and yet... "Theresa, I mean. You're not Theresa." Was he losing his mind?

"I most certainly am." A flirtatious light entered her eyes as she laughed.

It was all wrong. Her laugh was all wrong. Different. It wasn't husky, wasn't melodious. And there was no dimple at the corner of her mouth when she smiled, he realized suddenly. Had he imagined all of that? No, he couldn't have. He couldn't have imagined the color of her eyes, either. The ones he was looking into were clear water blue, not brilliant the way they had been.

Completely turned around and at a loss, Christopher ran a hand through his hair, staring at the woman in front of him. Maybe he was hallucinating?

"Theresa Cochran?" he repeated dumbly. He'd made love to the woman, absorbed every nuance of her body into his. Why did it feel as if he was looking into the face of a stranger?

Nodding, Theresa rounded her desk, a huntress scenting her prey. "Yes, I'm Theresa Cochran. I've never been Theresa Cochran more in my life."

T.J. opened the door that connected her office to Theresa's. She'd been doing some preliminary sketches on the next phase of advertising for MacAffee Toys and wanted to run it by Theresa. Lately, she didn't trust her judgment about anything. Her brain felt leaden.

"Theresa, I—" The inside of her mouth turned to dust. "Christopher." His name came out on a barely audible whisper.

When he turned to look at her, she saw the flicker of doubt, then recognition pass over his face.

No! The single word screamed in her brain. *Not like this.* She didn't want him finding out like this.

Flustered, miserable, T.J. backpedaled as fast as she could. "Mr. MacAffee, Theresa's told me so much about you. This is an honor, finally getting to meet you."

A brave smile pasted on her face, she stepped forward putting out her hand.

Christopher felt as if he'd just stumbled into a mirrored room in a carnival fun house. With a few changes here and there, Theresa and the woman greeting him looked enough alike to be twins.

In fact, if she just loosened her hair, the woman in the doorway… The look in her eyes…

As if in a trance, Christopher took the hand she

extended. He held it a moment longer than was necessary. Held it as he looked at her thoughtfully.

He saw the dimple at the corner of her mouth.

And then he knew.

10

"THERESA?"

Though in his mind, he knew, Christopher still couldn't make his heart believe it. Didn't want to believe that the woman he'd fallen in love with had deliberately duped him for some unknown reason. That would have made him the worst possible kind of fool.

Theresa felt as if she'd fallen into a foreign-language film where the subtitles had gotten scrambled. "No, I already told you, I'm Theresa."

"She is," T.J. told Christopher quietly. "I'm T.J." She couldn't draw her eyes away from his. They looked so dark, so forbidding. "Theresa, I'd like you to meet Christopher MacAffee."

The reason for the confusion had suddenly dawned on Theresa a moment before T.J. had said his name. The sinking sensation in the pit of Theresa's stomach widened at the confirmation.

"Oh, God."

Christopher didn't know what to say. What could he say? It was hard to form a coherent sentence while volcanoes were erupting all around him and the ground was shaking.

What the hell was going on here? Why had she lied to him about who she was? It didn't make any sense. All he knew was that she'd lied and that it hurt. Hurt like hell because he'd trusted her without reservations.

Her nerves knitted together furiously, and T.J. tried to keep a steady rein on them as she searched for a way to resolve this mess she found herself in.

Even as she did, she knew there was no way.

"Could you give us a minute, Theresa?" T.J. couldn't bring herself to look away, couldn't bring herself to look at anything except the deep, unreadable darkness in Christopher's eyes.

She should have told him, she thought in desperation. Somehow, she should have found a way to tell him. Now he was furious with her. But there still had to be a way to make him understand.

The tension in the room was almost physical, making it difficult to breathe.

"I can explain all this," Theresa began tentatively.

When he didn't look at her, Theresa laid a perfectly manicured, hot pink-tipped hand on his arm.

Christopher shrugged it off slowly, coldly. "I don't think anything needs to be explained. It's pretty evident." For whatever reason, she had played him for a fool. And he had helped her.

No, none of it was evident, T.J. thought fiercely. Whatever horrible thing he was thinking, she had to make him see that it wasn't true. That no harm had been intended. She couldn't stand having him look at her like that, as if he didn't know her. As if she'd done something awful to him.

"Theresa?" T.J. entreated her cousin.

Theresa understood and retreated. "I'll just be next

door if you need me." Unless she missed her guess, her cousin had more at stake here than she had.

It took Christopher a moment to get his emotions under control. Rage was a completely new feeling for him. As love had been before it. Funny how the same person roused both.

The room was so quiet, he could hear her breathing. "Interesting way you have of conducting business."

His voice was cold, impersonal. His eyes were like sharp knives, cutting out her heart. She wanted to speak, but couldn't.

"Do you and your cousin sleep with all your prospective clients?"

T.J.'s eyes widened as if she'd been physically slapped. She couldn't believe that he could say that to her. Whatever she'd expected to hear, it wasn't that. "That's not fair! I tried to tell you but you wouldn't listen."

"Fair?" Temper flashed in his eyes like a grease-laden pan bursting into flame. He saw her tremble as she stumbled a step backward. And then something seemed to snap to attention within her. She held her ground. He could have wrung her neck. "You're a hell of a one to talk about 'fair.' You used me, Theresa. Or T.J., or whoever the hell you really are." Bile rose in his mouth and left a bitter taste. As bitter a taste as her deception left. "I thought you were different, but you're like all the others." He supposed that made him naive. Thirty-three years old and he was behaving like some hayseed from the backwoods.

Her head jerked up. She had no idea what kind of people he'd dealt with, but she had a pretty good idea.

And she didn't like what he was saying. "Don't go lumping me in with people like that."

"Why?" he shouted into her face before he caught himself. He wasn't going to embarrass himself any more than he already had. Lowering his voice until it was a steely growl, he asked, "What makes you different?"

"I—"

He didn't want to hear elaborate excuses. He already knew how creative she could be. There were facts to deal with. "Did you or did you not sleep with me?"

T.J. felt as if she was being attacked. He wouldn't let her defend herself. "I did, but—"

"And do we or don't we now have a contract between us?"

This wasn't coming out right. He was twisting things around. What he was inferring wasn't true. She had to make him understand that. "Yes, but—"

That was his case, pure and simple. Pure and simple—that's what he'd thought she was, beneath the bravado. Talk about being a jerk—he took the prize. "Then how are you different?"

How could he ask? Didn't he know? "I don't do that sort of thing. I don't use my body to cement business relations."

He wanted to believe her. He couldn't believe her. "Oh, no?" The laugh was short, cruel. The sound cut right through her. "That's a little hard to believe. Don't forget, I was there."

T.J. clenched her hands into fists at her sides. She wanted to beat on him. To pound on his chest until she cracked that shield he had over it and freed his heart.

She lifted her chin defiantly. "I don't care what you believe." *Yes, yes, I do, damn you. How can you say these things to me? How could you make love with me and then say this?* "I just know what's true."

He turned from her and she grabbed his arm, jerking him around. The look he gave her almost turned her tongue to stone. But he had to hear this from her. He had to know.

"I didn't sleep with you because of the contracts, or because of business. It was just something that happened between us." He had to know that. Didn't he?

"Magic?" he said disdainfully.

She stared at him, dumbfounded. He was ridiculing her. Well, for her it *had* been magic.

"Yes, magic, for lack of a different word, or maybe it is the word. Magic, a spell. I don't know what came over me." Backing away from him, she threw up her hands as she began to pace about the office like a tiger searching for a way to escape out of its cage. "Damn it, I don't even kiss on the first date."

Tears were stinging her eyes and she drew in a deep breath, hoping that would somehow keep them from spilling out. She wouldn't let Christopher see her cry. He'd probably accuse her of using tears to make him feel guilty.

Swallowing, she turned to look at him, remembering the way it had been between them. Remembering the shimmering moment when she had thought he loved her. "It just felt as if you needed me—"

He had needed her. Or thought he had. But he refused to give her that satisfaction now. "Oh, then it was pity that had you making love to me."

She ignored the sarcasm. "And I needed you." Her eyes challenged him. "Now you can believe me or not, but I've never slept with anyone else except for Megan's father."

Megan. Something else she'd lied about. How many more lies were there? Probably too many to count. "Then she isn't your niece." There was no emotion in his voice and it was all the more chilling for that.

T.J. blew out a long, shaky breath. "No, she's my daughter."

Maybe, if he'd thought about it, he would have surmised as much. But he hadn't thought. Hadn't been able to think. She'd seemed to infiltrate every portion of his brain. Like a virus.

One he was damn well going to be inoculated against. "What else wasn't true?"

"Nothing." He didn't believe her. She could see it in his eyes. Why should he?

Why shouldn't he? she demanded more fiercely.

She was getting herself all tangled up. "Everything else was true. Everything I told you about the company." T.J. drew closer to him. "And everything that happened between us."

He had to believe that, she thought. He just had to. She couldn't bear it if he thought she'd lied to him about that.

He struggled with the temptation to crush her to him. God help him, even after all this, he still wanted her. Which made him an even bigger fool.

Christopher turned from her, from her haunted eyes

and from the scent of her hair that was driving him crazy with desire. "You'll forgive me if I cast a jaded eye on that."

Suddenly he had to get out of here. He started for the door.

Throwing herself into his path, T.J. made one more attempt. "Look, you were set to meet Theresa, insisted on it. 'Company policy,' we were told. Theresa really wanted your contract."

He felt his mouth twisting into a mocking sneer. "Apparently—"

Gaining momentum, T.J. wouldn't allow him to interrupt. "And then she was in a car accident—"

"Oh, please—" Did she think he was that naive? Car accident. Was that the best she could do? He would have given her more credit than that.

"She was," T.J. insisted. When he made a move to open the door, she placed her hand on his chest. Taking him by surprise, she managed to shove him back. "It was a minor accident, but the paramedics took her to the hospital and the doctor insisted on keeping her there for observation. She'd had a hard enough time scheduling this meeting with you and you were already on your way. She was afraid you'd be annoyed when she wasn't there and take your business to another company."

"Why didn't you just tell me she was in an accident?" That would have been the logical thing to do.

T.J. wished now that she had. "Theresa has a reputation for being flighty. She was afraid you'd just think she was putting you off."

Theresa, or T.J., he amended, had a point. He probably wouldn't have believed the excuse. He didn't think he did now.

She was losing him, she thought in desperation. "So she asked me to substitute for her."

He paused, reflecting. What was to keep her from lying further? Burned, he wasn't about to grab the red-hot skillet handle again so quickly. "Is that the story you two cooked up? Very creative."

Frustration clawed at her. What did it take for him to believe her?

"We didn't cook it up. It's true. You can check with the hospital. Harris Memorial. And if *you* hadn't gotten sick, you would have toured the offices, made your decision and left on the evening flight." Didn't he understand that? "But you did get sick and the rest just happened."

No, he wasn't going to be made a fool of twice. Served him right for believing in something as ethereal as love. "Conveniently."

What was the use? She wasn't getting through to him. Surrendering, T.J. backed away from the door. "You can say it happened any way you want to, but I just told you the truth."

"The truth." He echoed the word, mocking her. "New experience for you?"

How could she have given her heart to a man who didn't have one? T.J. dug her nails into the palms of her hand. She wasn't going to cry. She wasn't going to give Christopher the satisfaction of seeing her heart breaking in front of him.

She lifted a shoulder carelessly and let it fall. "You can believe me or not, the choice is yours. The facts are what I said they were. That, and one more thing."

Was she going to rub salt into the wounds she'd created and profess undying love? Did she really think he was that gullible? "And that is?"

She wanted to tell him she loved him. But what good would that do? He wouldn't believe her and that would leave her without the least bit of pride. Better that he never know.

Instead, she told him what had originally put her on this rocky road to nowhere. "That we are the best company for the job." T.J. thought of the figures she'd requested. The ones that had just arrived. "Marketing has been keeping tentative tabs on your sales. The bears are flying off the shelves."

They were. He knew that for a fact. His own people had called him with the news just before he'd boarded the plane. It was one of the things he'd wanted to tell her. Along with something else, something very important. Something that no longer mattered.

He was grateful he'd found everything out before he'd made a complete fool of himself.

It was cold comfort to him.

His eyes searched her face. He thought of the way he'd rushed here to see her. She'd probably have a good laugh over that, wouldn't she? "It was just business with you, wasn't it?"

If he really thought that, maybe she didn't want to be with him after all.

The hell you don't.

She shut the voice, and her feelings, out. Somehow she was going to get through this. And past it. She had to.

Lifting her chin, she answered, "There are people

depending on the company for jobs. Families with bills to pay, kids to send to school.''

She was giving him his answer, he thought. She was saying yes.

''Save it for a card commercial,'' he snapped. How could she? How could she have used him this way? Didn't she think her company could stand up on its own merits? Or did she think that he was so feeble-minded as to be led around by his desire? ''I would have given the contracts to you, anyway. You didn't have to sleep with me.''

The sanctimonious bastard. ''No,'' she agreed impassively. ''I didn't.''

Couldn't he tell that she cared, that she'd fallen for him the moment she'd seen him walking in her direction? That she wasn't the type who would just give her body for the fun of it? Never mind that he was supposed to think she was Theresa, he should have *known.* Making love with her, he should have known.

But he didn't.

Her mouth hardened. ''Consider it a bonus.'' She squared her shoulders and looked past his head. ''Now if you'll excuse me, I have some small children to lead astray.''

His eyes bore small holes into her. What the hell gave her the right to be sarcastic when he was the wounded party?

''Fine,'' he bit off. As an afterthought, he threw the manila envelope on Theresa's desk. ''There are the contracts.''

The envelope fell on the desk with a thud and then slid off onto the floor. She didn't even look in its direction.

"You're staying with the company?" She would have thought that would have been his final revenge, to pull his business.

"Sure." The laugh was without humor. "As you pointed out, the bears are flying off the shelves. I'd be a fool to turn my back on good business. And I've already been enough of a fool, haven't I?"

And with that, he walked out of the office. The slam of the door vibrated into her very soul.

She was still standing there, staring at the door, her hands clenched at her sides, when Theresa reentered. She picked up the manila envelope and put it on the desk. Quietly she crossed to T.J. and placed her arms around her cousin.

"Are you all right?" she asked softly.

No, she wasn't. She was never going to be all right again. T.J. wiped the tears away with the back of her hand.

"Sure, I'm fine. Just fine." Her voice nearly broke but she managed to get it under control again. "I made love with him when I was playing you."

She didn't know why she was even saying it. Theresa had probably heard everything. All of L.A. had probably heard.

A soft, sympathetic smile played on Theresa's lips. "Did I enjoy it?"

T.J. shut her eyes for a moment before answering. "Yes. Very much."

Theresa's heart ached for T.J. It wasn't often her sympathies were stirred, but a stone would have ached for T.J. right now. She brushed back a loose strand from T.J.'s face. It was flushed, she noted, as if T.J. was trying very hard not to cry.

The streaks along her cheeks gleamed.

"By the look on your face, I'd say I enjoyed the week I had with him more than the week I had here."

T.J. looked at her cousin sharply, her feelings exposed, raw. "This isn't funny, Theresa."

"No, I can see where it wouldn't be." Theresa gave her shoulder a little squeeze. "I can go after him for you and try to make it right."

She had no idea what she'd say to the man, but she'd come up with something. She'd never seen T.J. so upset, not even when she discovered that Peter had been cheating on her.

But T.J. shook her head, stopping her before she could leave. "Don't bother. Nothing is going to make this right."

"I can be very persuasive if I have to be."

T.J. knew what that meant. That was all she needed, to have Theresa "persuade" Christopher. "Not with him you won't."

Theresa raised her hands in surrender. "Hands off, I promise." She dropped them to her side, growing serious. "I just want to see you smile again."

"I will," T.J. promised. "In time." But not anytime soon.

Theresa had her doubts. She glanced toward the door. Maybe if she tried to talk some sense into Christopher, tell him that it was all her fault.

"I can—"

T.J. didn't want Theresa interfering. This was between her and Christopher. "No."

Theresa wasn't accustomed to being voted down. "But—"

This time, T.J. placed a restraining hand on Theresa's arm. She was firm on this. "No, Theresa. If he comes back, he comes back on his own, not because you bent his arm. Or any other part of him," she added pointedly. She released Theresa's arm. "I told him the truth. That should have been enough."

If he cared about her half as much as she had about him, T.J. thought, it would have been.

Theresa's expression was skeptical. "In all fairness to him, how is he supposed to know which 'truth' to believe? You did lie to him."

So now she was taking his side? "Because you asked me to."

Theresa shook her head. Men were very sensitive creatures when it came to their egos, no matter what they let on. "He doesn't care about that part. You lied to him once and maybe he's afraid of believing you now. Maybe he's afraid you're still lying."

It made sense, but she didn't want sense. She wanted Christopher. She wanted him to have faith in her no matter what. "He should know the difference."

"Why?"

T.J. avoided Theresa's eyes. "Because people in love do."

Theresa took her face in one hand and looked into T.J.'s eyes. Love. She'd had no idea. She'd thought only passion had been involved. This made it a great deal worse. "That bad?"

T.J. drew her head back, and then sighed. "Yes, that bad."

Theresa sank down, leaning against her desk. "Oh, T.J., if I'd known this was going to happen, I would have never asked you to take my place."

"Why?" Still smarting, T.J. looked at her. "Because he's handsome and you would have wanted him for yourself?" She was accustomed to that. Theresa had gone after someone she'd cared about more than once and whisked him away before she'd ever had a chance. It was in Theresa's nature to be competitive when it came to men.

Theresa took no offense. "No, because you're hurting and I don't want you to be."

T.J. looked at her cousin sharply. The smile came to her lips slowly as realization set in. "You mean that, don't you?"

"Yes." Theresa rose to her feet again. "I might be a world-class witch sometimes, but you're my cousin and I do love you." She laid an arm around T.J.'s shoulders. "I don't want anything to hurt you."

"Thanks."

Theresa bit her lip. She hated for it to just end this way. Particularly if T.J. loved the man. "Are you sure there isn't anything I can do?"

"No, there isn't anything anyone can do. Not now." *Not ever,* T.J. added silently.

"Do you want to go home? Pamper yourself? Soak in a hot tub? Make a dart board with his face on it?"

T.J. laughed, a tiny spark returning. All of those were Theresa's methods of dealing with things, not hers. Besides, she didn't have a photograph of Christopher that she could use.

Nothing but the image in her mind.

"No, I want to work." T.J. looked at the drawings she'd placed on Theresa's desk a hundred years ago, before the world had crumbled. "Here." She spread them out. "What do you think of these?"

Theresa looked at her skeptically. "T.J., now?"

"Now." She paused. "Please."

"All right." Theresa nodded and looked down at the drawings.

11

IT HAD BEEN, T.J. thought as she dragged herself out of her office, one of the longest days she could remember ever putting in. It hadn't been because of the number of hours she had been here. It was a standard eight-to-five day as far as that went. No, the problem was with the date itself. Valentine's Day.

This one had been particularly bad for her.

Maybe it was just her imagination working overtime, but everywhere she turned, it seemed as if thoughts of Christopher would assault her. They would race through her mind unannounced, making her remember. Making her ache.

Today was supposed to have been special for them. Today Christopher was supposed to have returned from San Jose and taken her out for the evening. Perhaps even given her a card. Some silly little thing she would have cherished forever.

Except now, of course, he wouldn't. They wouldn't ever see each another again.

The hell with him. The hell with everything. T.J. mumbled a good-night to Heidi and kept walking.

At one point, the day had become so hard to endure that T.J. had decided to leave early. She never got the chance. Today, of all days, Theresa had waylaid her with a project. She'd been forced to remain until now, working out details and watching a parade of flowers and gifts arrive for Theresa.

Didn't matter, T.J. told herself, walking down the hall. She didn't need any of that. Tomorrow this fanfare would be over and she could just continue with her life. Alone. With Megan, she corrected silently.

But alone where it counted.

Damn him for ever coming into her life.

She had to stop dwelling on him. It was over. Over almost before it was begun.

No, she amended, punching the down button on the wall. That wasn't really true. It had been begun, all right. With a parade and confetti and a fifty-piece brass band marching down the center of town. And ended, she thought sadly, with the same amount of noise.

She'd hoped.

Wished.

T.J. pressed her lips together as the elevator arrived, banking down her emotions. Emotions that threatened to run riot through her. There was no point in raking herself over the coals about this anymore. Life went forward, not back.

Even on Valentine's Day.

The silvery doors of the elevator yawned opened. Stepping forward, she was forced to quickly step back again. There was a forest of plump red roses fairly choking out of a long white vase directly in her path. All she could see of the person carrying them were jean-clad legs and hands attached to the slim column of alabaster.

Another delivery. She sighed. *Some of us have it and some of us don't.*

"Second door from the end," T.J. mechanically instructed. More booty for Theresa. Flowers, candy and an array of boxes she could only assume were lingerie had been arriving for her cousin all day.

"Gee, thanks," the profusion of roses responded.

T.J and the deliveryman then did a sashay that looked like a mating dance, exchanging places until T.J. was the one on the elevator and the deliveryman was out in the hall.

Leaning over, T.J. pressed the first-floor button. As the doors closed, she saw the deliveryman craning his neck around the side of the arrangement he held as he tried to make his way down the hall without a mishap.

Didn't matter if he had one, T.J. shrugged to herself. One bouquet more or less, Theresa would never notice its absence. She'd given up wondering how Theresa managed to know so many unattached males.

T.J. banked down her sour mood. It wasn't fair to be annoyed with Theresa. Theresa couldn't help it if she attracted men like honey did bees. And bears.

The thought of bears resurrected an image of Christopher in her mind.

No, she upbraided herself. No more Christopher. Ever. Some were meant to have romance in their lives and some weren't.

Until now, it really hadn't bothered her that much, apart from the hype of Valentine's Day.

Hype, she reminded herself tersely as she made her way through the parking lot, that she was as guilty of promoting as the next person.

Maybe more so. After all, she'd been the one to push MacAffee Toys into the holiday.

She couldn't chastise herself about that. It was what she was paid for. To have ideas. T.J. got into her car and slammed the door. Hard.

Right now, the wrong ones were plaguing her no matter how she tried to block them.

Annoyed with herself, T.J. turned up the radio.

"And now, this one is for all you lovers out there. Elvis, singing '*Love Me Tender*,'" the disc jockey announced as she pulled out of the lot.

Muttering under her breath, T.J. shoved the first handy tape into her tape deck.

A deep male voice began singing that it was beginning to look a lot like Christmas. T.J. left it on.

THE DRIVE HOME was virtually accomplished on automatic pilot. Under oath, T.J. couldn't have said how she'd gotten there. She just had. Mercifully intact.

With a flick of her wrist, she aimed the garage door opener at the closed dove gray door. The hinges on either side creaked as it opened to admit her.

Maybe, she mused driving in, just this once she'd take a page out of Theresa's book. She'd pamper herself with a bubble bath right after she put Megan to bed.

A really hot bubble bath, T.J. decided. With any luck, she'd purge Christopher out of her system once and for all.

He didn't belong there anyway.

Getting out of the car, she saw a flicker of pink out of the corner of her eye. Curious, she walked around the back of her car and looked out.

There were rose petals strewn in her driveway. Pink

rose petals. The breeze had ruffled some of them, but from the looks of it, they formed a trail.

A trail of rose petals?

Puzzled, she followed them and found that they led to her front door.

She would have said that Megan was responsible, except that there were no roses in her garden and the petals looked as if they had been deliberately arranged to form a path to her door.

T.J. couldn't begin to make heads or tails out of it. Maybe it was someone's bizarre idea of a joke. If that was the case, she was far too tired to be amused. She still didn't understand why Theresa had insisted she remain until five. Theresa was usually the one ushering her out the door if she showed the slightest inclination to leave early.

Who knew? Who knew anything, T.J. thought irritably. All she wanted was for today to be over.

Unlocking the front door, T.J. discovered that the lights were out. They shouldn't have been. But the only illumination in the house was a small, eerie light coming from beyond the living room.

T.J. caught her lower lip between her teeth. This was getting to be really strange.

Venturing in, T.J. looked around. Nothing. No one. Where was everybody?

"Cecilia? Megan? I'm home." She paused, waiting. "Where are you?"

There was no answer.

Nerves began to manifest themselves. Her purse slipped from her slick fingers. As she bent down to pick it up, she saw that the rose petals were inside the house, too. Leading away from the door.

Heart quickening, T.J. had no choice but to continue to follow the trail. It extended through the living room into the dining room, where it stopped abruptly at the table.

It didn't even look like her table. There was a fine white lace tablecloth spread over the cherrywood top and it was set for two. The light that had guided her through the house was coming from two tall, tapering candles set in silver stands.

A light scent of berries was in the air.

Rather than a covered dish containing dinner, in the center of the table, between the two candlesticks, was a small, white teddy bear. His clasped paws were beribboned to help him hold on to a velvet box.

Just like in the commercial.

It was a joke.

Angry now, T.J. fisted her hands at her waist. She raised her voice. "All right, Theresa, this isn't funny." Her voice echoed back to her. It was all she heard.

Theresa had been exceptionally kind to her today, as if she understood what she was going through. But this sort of thing was her speed. It had Theresa written all over it. And she was carrying the joke too far.

"Enough." T.J. looked around the empty room. Unease nudged a place for itself beside her anger. Why was Theresa doing this? It had to be Theresa. Who else would have gone to this trouble for a prank? "Come out, come out wherever you are. Game over. Go home."

Still no one.

"All right, I'll see this through," she called out.

"I'm reaching for the bear." T.J. squeezed it, just the way the woman in the commercial had.

Instead of "I wuv you," the bear said, quite audibly, "Flip my switch."

Surprised, T.J. stared down at the small bear. "Is that anything like ring my chimes?" T.J. shook her head. "My God, I'm talking to a stuffed bear."

But she turned it around and found the tiny switch. Flipping it, she heard a click and then the sound of a man's voice.

Christopher's voice.

She dropped the bear. It continued talking.

"Forgive me. I've been an idiot."

T.J. scooped up the bear, then looked around, her heart slamming against her rib cage. "Christopher?"

Was he here? Had he come back to see her? Why—?

"Right here."

She swung around. He was standing in the doorway behind her. He hadn't been there a second ago. There was no time to think, only react. T.J. dropped the bear again and flung herself into his arms.

Oh, God, he thought he'd never be this happy again. For a moment, watching her, he'd been afraid that it was too late. But it wasn't. She was in his arms and it wasn't too late.

Lowering his mouth to hers, Christopher kissed her, kissed her like a man back from the dead. Because that's what he was. Back from the dead. The living dead. Without her, he'd only been marking time. He just didn't know it until she'd entered his life. And then left it again.

"Wait a minute." Wedging her hands between

them, T.J. pushed him back. She searched his face for an explanation. "What's going on here?"

"I'm keeping our Valentine date." *And my sanity,* he added silently.

"What date?" she asked incredulously. Had he forgotten what he'd said? "The last I saw of you, you were walking out of my life as fast as you could go. What happened?"

"I had time to think and came to my senses. I did nothing but think. Of you." He coaxed T.J. back into his arms. He never wanted her to be out of reach again. "No matter how hard I tried not to, there you were, inside of every report I read, within every dream I had, sitting in on every meeting I tried to conduct."

His mouth curved as his eyes tried to absorb her. He'd been so afraid that he had lost her.

"You might say I was haunted. My father always old me to face up to whatever I was running from." t was the one good piece of advice the older man had given him. "So here I am."

T.J.'s eyes narrowed. She didn't want to let herself get carried away. She was afraid to. "So this is a howdown?"

"No, it's a show up. I've showed up the way I was upposed to."

He paused, debating telling her. But there were gong to be no more secrets between them. That meant n both sides. Still, if he told her, she would know e went on doubting her story until it was confirmed y outside sources. He knew that might not go down well.

Christopher took his chances. "I called the hospital."

"Hospital?"

He nodded, then recited the information he'd been given. "One Theresa Cochran had been admitted overnight the day I arrived in L.A."

Finally, he had to believe her. She couldn't have very well bribed hospital personnel to lie for her. "Why would I have lied about that?"

The answer was simple; at least it had been for him at the time. "Because you lied about who you were."

Were they going to go over old ground after all? "I already told you, there was a reason for that."

He didn't want to argue about that. Or about anything, ever again.

"Yes, you did, and I guess, seeing it from your point of view, you might have expected me to be inflexible." A smile spread over his face as he remembered making love with her. "Instead of the flexible man I turned out to be."

She could read his mind. It wasn't hard. "And agile. Don't forget agile."

It was going to be okay, he thought. He hadn't blown it. "I might need a refresher course when it comes to that."

She couldn't think of anything she'd rather do more. But they weren't alone. Or were they? "Where are Megan and Cecilia?"

Meticulously, Christopher had taken care of everything. "Theresa's. I asked if they could stay there for a while." He smiled into her eyes. "Perhaps the night."

"Theresa's?" T.J. echoed. "Does she know about this?"

"She knows."

He knew he wouldn't be able to pull off this apology alone. He'd needed an inside accomplice. Theresa had seemed the likely choice. Once contacted, Theresa had been more than eager to help. She'd been the one to suggest Megan and Cecilia remain at her house overnight.

"And she didn't say anything to me?" Theresa could never keep a secret.

"I asked her not to." The woman had promised, probably afraid that he would pull the contract if she didn't keep her word. It didn't matter. All that mattered was having the woman he loved here in his arms like this. "Did you receive my flowers?"

T.J. laughed. They could hardly be called flowers now. "All down the driveway, all over the house."

It took him a second to understand. "No, not the petals. I mean the flowers I sent to the office. I timed the delivery for just when you were leaving. Three dozen long-stemmed roses."

She thought of the huge bouquet that had gotten off the elevator and she groaned. Her first flowers for Valentine's Day and she had given them away. "I sent them to Theresa."

Maybe he wasn't home free after all. "You didn't want them?"

"No, I mean, I didn't know they were for me. I thought they were for Theresa. Flowers and things have been arriving for her all day." T.J. shrugged helplessly. "I'm sorry." More than Christopher could possibly guess, she thought. "I figured it was just another one of her admirers."

She looked so upset, he kissed away the furrow between her brows. "It wasn't. It was one of your admirers."

"Admirer," she corrected. "No plural." She raised her eyes to his. "And do you? Admire?" she added.

He grinned, his eyes touching her. Loving her. "I intend to. Closely," he whispered. *For the rest of my life.* Christopher held her against him, looking down into her face. A face he'd missed so much. "So, what are you doing Valentine's Day?"

She laughed. That was an odd question. "I'm spending it here with you now."

She'd misunderstood. Not that he could blame her. "No, I meant Valentine's Day 2010."

T.J. blinked. He wasn't making any sense. "What?"

Releasing her, he crossed to where she had dropped the bear and picked it up. He handed the stuffed animal to her. "You're not finished with the bear."

T.J. cupped her hand around the gift. "He has more to say?"

"He has more to give." Christopher indicated the box in the bear's paws. If it hadn't been wrapped up so tightly, it would have fallen when she'd dropped the bear. He saw her hands were trembling as she untied the red ribbon.

"How did you get him to sound like you?" She fumbled with the knot.

Christopher was tempted to help her with the ribbon. Instead, he shoved his hands into his pockets. "I had the designers rig a tiny microrecorder in his stomach. I thought 'I wuv you' just wouldn't do the trick this time.''

It would have, she thought. T.J. finally managed to get the ribbon off. She placed the bear on the table. If fell on its back. Taking a deep breath, she opened the box. Her eyes stung. Oh, God, she couldn't cry now.

''It's a ring,'' she whispered in disbelief.

''I know.'' The next few seconds would tell him if he'd been a fool or not. ''I picked it out.''

She raised her eyes to his. She couldn't believe—refused to believe—''For me?''

He raised one shoulder and let it drop carelessly. ''It's too large for the bear.''

T.J. stared at it again. ''But it's an engagement ring.''

She wasn't taking it out of the box. Why wasn't she taking it out of the box? Was she going to turn him down after all?

''People usually give them when they get engaged.'' Christopher took a deep breath. It was time to go all the way. ''That is, if you want to be engaged to a jerk.''

''No, I don't.'' T.J. paused, looking up at him. She saw the look of bewildered disappointment in his eyes. He didn't understand, she realized. ''I want to be engaged to you.''

Relief flooded him. Taking the ring out of the box, he slipped it on her finger. Christopher gathered her into his arms again. It *was* going to be all right. ''You know, I should have gone with my first instincts.''

She couldn't help it. T.J. extended her hand and

watched the candlelight dance on the diamond, making it catch fire. "Which were?"

He laughed when he saw what she was doing. She made him think of a little girl with a precious new trinket. He couldn't wait to shower her with more "trinkets."

"That you were the woman I'd been looking for. Smart, funny, warm. Not to mention a terrific kisser." He thought for a second, growing serious. "I suppose it was easier not to believe it. It's a scary thing."

"What is?"

His eyes touched hers. "Happiness."

T.J. laced her arms around his neck. "Want to be scared together?"

"I'd love it." He brushed her lips with a kiss, whetting his appetite. "And you."

"Nice to know," she murmured. Tempting him, she leaned her body into his. "Because I'd hate to think it was a one-way street."

He wanted to hear it. Needed to hear it. "Then you do love me?"

"Of course I love you." Her eyes were teasing him. "Do you think I go around accepting talking bears from just anyone?"

"No, I guess maybe you don't." He couldn't remember when he'd been this happy. "Never" came to mind. "Happy Valentine's Day."

Just as he lowered his mouth to hers, she asked, "Say it."

Puzzled, he drew his head back. "Say what?"

"My name." He hadn't really called her by her name, except for that one time. She wanted to hear the sound of it on his lips without anger. "Say my name."

"T.J." She didn't look like a T.J. T.J.'s were cool, efficient. They weren't warm, giving women. They didn't flow through their lovers' hands like heated mercury. "You know, I like the sound of 'darling' better." The smile faded from his face, to be replaced with a look of love. Everlasting love. "Happy Valentine's Day, darling," he whispered against her mouth.

It was hard to imagine a heart singing, but hers did. This had turned out to be one hell of a day after all. "Happy Valentine's Day."

And it was. If asked, the stuffed animal on the table could bear witness to that. The record button had accidentally been turned on when it fell.

Silhouette's newest series

YOURS TRULY

Love when you least expect it.

Where the written word plays a vital role in uniting couples—you're guaranteed a fun and exciting read every time!

Look for Marie Ferrarella's upcoming Yours Truly, *Traci on the Spot*, in March 1997.

Here's a special sneak preview....

1

Morgan Brigham slowly set down his coffee cup on the kitchen table and stared at the comic strip in the center of his paper. It was nestled in among approximately twenty others that were spread out across two pages. But this was the only one he made a point of reading faithfully each morning at breakfast.

This was the only one that mirrored *her* life.

He read each panel twice, as if he couldn't trust his own eyes. But he could. It was there, in black and white.

Morgan folded the paper slowly, thoughtfully, his mind not on his task. So Traci was getting engaged.

The realization gnawed at the lining of his stomach. He hadn't a clue as to why.

He had even less of a clue why he did what he did next.

Abandoning his coffee, now cool, and the newspaper, and ignoring the fact that this was going to make him late for the office, Morgan went to get a sheet of stationery from the den.

He didn't have much time.

Traci Richardson stared at the last frame she had just drawn. Debating, she glanced at the creature sprawled out on the kitchen floor.

"What do you think, Jeremiah? Too blunt?"

The dog, part bloodhound, part mutt, idly looked up from his rawhide bone at the sound of his name. Jeremiah gave her a look she felt free to interpret as ambivalent.

"Fine help you are. What if Daniel actually reads this and puts two and two together?"

Not that there was all that much chance that the man who had proposed to her, the very prosperous and busy Dr. Daniel Thane, would actually see the comic strip she drew for a living. Not unless the strip was taped to a bicuspid he was examining. Lately Daniel had gotten so busy he'd stopped reading anything but the morning headlines of the *Times*.

Still, you never knew. "I don't want to hurt his feelings," Traci continued, using Jeremiah as a sounding board. "It's just that Traci is overwhelmed by Donald's proposal and, see, she thinks the ring is going to swallow her up." To prove her point, Traci held up the drawing for the dog to view.

This time, he didn't even bother to lift his head.

Traci stared moodily at the small velvet box on the kitchen counter. It had sat there since Daniel had asked her to marry him last Sunday. Even if Daniel never read her comic strip, he was going to suspect something eventually. The very fact that she hadn't grabbed the ring from his hand and slid it onto her finger should have told him that she had doubts about their union.

Traci sighed. Daniel was a catch by any definition. So what was her problem? She kept waiting to be struck by that sunny ray of happiness. Daniel said he wanted to take care of her, to fulfill her every wish. And he was even willing to let her think about it before she gave him her answer.

Guilt nibbled at her. She should be dancing up and down, not wavering like a weather vane in a gale.

Pronouncing the strip completed, she scribbled her signature in the corner of the last frame and then sighed. Another week's work put to bed. She glanced at the pile of mail on the counter. She'd been bringing it in steadily from the mailbox since Monday, but the stack had gotten no farther than her kitchen. Sorting letters seemed the least heinous of all the annoying chores that faced her.

Traci paused as she noted a long envelope. Morgan Brigham. Why would Morgan be writing to her?

Curious, she tore open the envelope and quickly scanned the short note inside.

Dear Traci,

I'm putting the summerhouse up for sale. Thought you might want to come up and see it one more time before it goes up on the block. Or make a bid for it yourself. If memory serves, you once said you wanted to buy it. Either way, let me know. My number's on the card.

Take care,

Morgan

P.S. Got a kick out of *Traci on the Spot* this week.

Traci folded the letter. He read her strip. She hadn't known that. A feeling of pride silently coaxed a smile to her lips. After a beat, though, the rest of his note seeped into her consciousness. He was selling the house.

The summerhouse. A faded white building with brick trim. Suddenly, memories flooded her mind. Long, lazy afternoons that felt as if they would never end.

Morgan.

She looked at the far wall in the family room. There was a large framed photograph of her and Morgan standing before the summerhouse. Traci and Morgan. Morgan and Traci. Back then, it seemed their lives had been permanently intertwined. A bittersweet feeling of loss passed over her.

Traci quickly pulled the telephone over to her on the counter and tapped out the number on the keypad.

* * * * *

LOVE & LAUGHTER™

MOTHER KNOWS BEST —MAYBE!

These matchmaking moms have had enough of their happy-to-be-single kids. How is a respectable woman to become a grandmother unless her offspring cooperates? There's nothing to be done except to get the kids down the aisle, even if they go kicking and screaming all the way!

Plans are made, schemes hatched, plots unraveled. Let the love and laughter begin!

Enjoy Matchmaking Moms, beginning with:

#15 A ROYAL PAIN, March 1997
by Ruth Jean Dale

#17 ONE MOM TOO MANY, April 1997
by Vicki Lewis Thompson

Watch for more Matchmaking Moms in the months ahead!

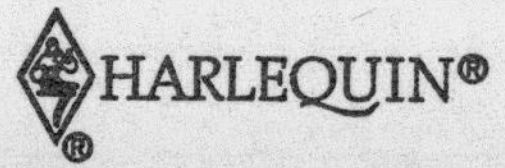

Free Gift Offer

With a Free Gift proof-of-purchase from any Harlequin® book, you can receive a beautiful cubic zirconia pendant.

This stunning marquise-shaped stone is a genuine cubic zirconia—accented by an 18" gold tone necklace.
(Approximate retail value $19.95)

Send for yours today... compliments of HARLEQUIN®

ɔ receive your free gift, a cubic zirconia pendant, send us one original proof-of-ırchase, photocopies not accepted, from the back of any Harlequin Romance®, arlequin Presents®, Harlequin Temptation®, Harlequin Superromance®, Harlequin trigue®, Harlequin American Romance®, or Harlequin Historicals® title available in ɛbruary, March or April at your favorite retail outlet, together with the Free Gift rtificate, plus a check or money order for $1.65 U.S./$2.15 CAN. (do not send cash) to ver postage and handling, payable to Harlequin Free Gift Offer. We will send you the ecified gift. Allow 6 to 8 weeks for delivery. Offer good until April 30, 1997, or while antities last. Offer valid in the U.S. and Canada only.

Free Gift Certificate

ame: ____________________

ldress: ____________________

y: ______________ State/Province: ______________ Zip/Postal Code: ______

ail this certificate, one proof-of-purchase and a check or money order for postage d handling to: HARLEQUIN FREE GIFT OFFER 1997. In the U.S.: 3010 Walden enue, P.O. Box 9071, Buffalo NY 14269-9057. In Canada: P.O. Box 604, Fort Erie, ıtario L2Z 5X3.

FREE GIFT OFFER **084-KEZ**

ONE PROOF-OF-PURCHASE

To collect your fabulous FREE GIFT, a cubic zirconia pendant, you must include this original proof-of-purchase for each gift with the properly completed Free Gift Certificate.

084-KEZ

Four generations of independent women...
Four heartwarming, romantic stories of the West...
Four incredible authors...

Fern Michaels
Jill Marie Landis
Dorsey Kelley
Chelley Kitzmiller

Saddle up with Heartbreak Ranch, an outstanding Western collection that will take you on a whirlwind trip through four generations and the exciting, romantic adventures of four strong women who have inherited the ranch from Bella Duprey, famed Barbary Coast madam.

Available in March,
wherever Harlequin books are sold.

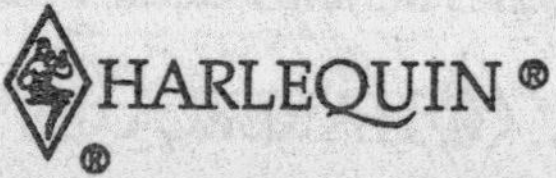

Look us up on-line at: http://www.romance.net HTBK